The Mysterious Messenger

The MYSTERIOUS MESSENGER

Gilbert Ford

Christy Ottaviano Books

Henry Holt and Company

New York

Henry Holt and Company
Publishers since 1866
120 Broadway, New York, NY 10271
mackids.com
Henry Holt® is a registered trademark of Henry Holt and Company, LLC

Our books may be purchased for promotional, educational, or business use.
Please contact your local bookseller or the Macmillan Corporate
and Premium Sales Department at (800) 221-7945 x5442 or
by email at MacmillanSpecialMarkets@macmillan.com.

Library of Congress Control Number: 2020905443

ISBN 978-1-250-20567-4

First edition, 2020 / Designed by Katie Klimowicz
Printed in the United States of America by LSC Communications,
Harrisonburg, Virginia
1 3 5 7 9 10 8 6 4 2

TO MY DAD & GRANDAD,
WHOSE NAME I SHARE

The Mysterious Messenger

1
The Spirits Visit

pirit of the late Robert Fisher," whispered Maria's mother from the other side of the wall, "I summon you to this table on behalf of the dear wife you left behind so many years ago."

Maria shifted her weight in the walk-in closet of her mother's bedroom. The air was stale, with musty fur coats that clung to hangers high above. She brushed her curly hair from her face and pressed her eye to the holes that ornamented the grate looking into the parlor.

A tiny candle pierced the darkness in the next room, illuminating the dusty magenta of her mother's turban and her thin hands above a crystal ball. Beside her sat an elderly woman wearing glasses. Her hair was pulled into a white bun that glowed in the light.

"For it is I, Madame Destine Russo, who begs you to inhabit me," whispered Maria's mother. The psychic shut her eyes and froze, the stillness interrupted by the rustling of a parrot perched on her mink shoulder.

Madame Destine's eyes popped open. "Come!" she said, slamming her fist onto the card table. "Speak to your dear Marilyn!"

The parrot beat its wings before settling. Feathers floated around the two women seated at the table while Madame Destine's eyes rolled back. Then her body spasmed, shaking her pale hands so that her bracelets rattled against the table.

Maria pulled away from the grate, her heart pounding. Even now, as an eleven-year-old who'd been part of the act since she could talk, she feared something would go wrong. Her fingers fumbled over the switch until she turned it. "Don't mess this up!" she told herself.

The blades of the fan spun behind Maria until they gained momentum. Then she ducked, allowing the cool breeze to shoot through the grate and into the parlor.

Very slowly, the wind chimes sang a sad spirit song and the loose hairs on the old woman's bun stirred under the flickering candlelight. Pipes clanged. Faint moans echoed deep inside the apartment.

Madame Destine shook before the startled old woman, their shadows running across the velvet curtains blocking the daylight.

Then Madame Destine froze again, letting out a soft whimper. Gradually, she tumbled onto the table, her head slamming beside her crystal ball with a loud thud.

The parrot flapped his wings again before settling on top of her turban.

Maria switched off the fan. Then she pressed her eye against the grate, looking for directions from her mother.

"Madame Destine?" said Mrs. Fisher, stretching her neck over the lifeless mound. "Are you okay?"

Maria rolled her eyes. Boy, was this old lady gullible. Although the scam changed from time to time, she knew what would soon follow. That widow's wedding ring would be their meal ticket until the next naive victim arrived in their apartment looking for answers.

The widow shivered, turning her head around the parlor as if to look for signs of life. Finally, she grabbed her purse and shot up from her folding chair.

"Marilyn!" said a guttural voice.

The old woman stopped, then grabbed at her heart.

Madame Destine's face rose from the table. "Mariiilyn," she said in the same deep voice. "My sweet Maaaaaarilyn."

Mrs. Fisher fell back into her chair and swallowed. "Oh, Robert?" she gasped. "Is it you? Is it REALLY you?"

"Marilyn, how I've missed you!" said Madame Destine.

"Oh, sweetie, it's been twenty years, but not a day's gone by that I've not thought of you," said Mrs. Fisher.

"Sweeeet Marilyn," said Maria's mother, her eyebrow arching above one open eye. "I miss the world of the living. It's so cooooold here without you."

"My Robby, I'll soon be joining you, I'm sure of that!"

"But, Marilyn," said Madame Destine quickly. "There's JUST one thing you must do before you join me. Just one favor I ask of you."

"I'll do whatever you want. Just say it!"

Madame Destine's eyes darted sideways at the large diamond ring on Marilyn Fisher's finger. "Oh, Marilyn," she said, and tossed her head back. "It's been two decades since we've been together. Do you still wear the wedding ring I gave you the day we made our vows?"

Mrs. Fisher glanced down at her hand and forced a smile. "I still wear the ring with pride, my love. I'll always be your girl." Her chin trembled.

Maria pushed away from the grate. Then she laid her head back onto the worn pillow on her tiny mattress. She propped her Converse sneakers against the wall before mouthing the words that came from her mother in the other room. "You must part with material possessions before you join me in the next world!" Maria waved the way she knew Madame Destine would, with palms out and fingers spread apart.

Kerthump!

A fur coat fell on Maria's head. She pushed the moth-eaten lining away from her and stood up in the cramped closet that also served as her bedroom. She grabbed the coat covering her gray blanket and tiptoed around her mattress, stepping on pens, paper, and library books.

"Ouch!" Maria said under her breath. She'd hit her head

on the hanging light bulb. Maria steadied it before placing the fur back on its hanger nestled with her mother's clothes. The fan pointing at the grate took up most of the real estate, and Maria had to carefully ease back into position without knocking it over.

"I ask that you donate your ring, the symbol of our love and happy marriage, to the Brooklyn Urban Youth Initiative for Tomorrow," said the deep voice of Madame Destine in the next room.

"TOMORROW! TOMORROW!" screeched the parrot.

"Silence, Houdini!" snapped Madame Destine.

Maria imagined Mrs. Fisher must be wondering why on earth her husband's spirit wanted her to give her ring to charity, but she knew her mother had already solved that riddle.

"Our marriage produced no children, Marilyn. My only regret was not having a child to look after."

"But, sweetie? You hated children. We talked about this."

"And THAT is my biggest regret!" said Madame Destine, a little too soon and way too sharply.

"Well," said the voice of Mrs. Fisher, "I suppose I could write a check. I would have to research the organization to make sure it was—"

"No!" boomed Madame Destine, slamming her fist on the table. "It must be *your* ring. It must be *this* organization."

The pipes clanged in the apartment, and soft moans

echoed in the hallway before the signal had been given. Maria slapped her forehead. "Oh, you've done it again, Mr. Fox!" she mumbled. She rolled off her mattress and turned on the fan so the candles could flicker and the wind chimes could whine in the next room. She listened for her mother's bracelets to jangle, followed by the loud thud of her head striking the table. Then Maria cut off the fan and fell back on her mattress.

The house was silent.

Maria shut her eyes and cleared her mind in the stiff, musty air of the closet. She tried not to think of her mother and her scam, or Mr. Fox coming in too early with the eerie sounds. She pushed how they were conning a helpless widow to the back of her mind. She even ignored the pain in her stomach. It had been twenty-four hours since Maria had eaten.

As she let her mind go blank, she settled into stillness. And ever so faintly, her fingers began to tingle—the same tingle of lip balm on cracked lips or the first bite of minty gum in a stale mouth. She felt his fresh, comforting grip hold her hand. Although she'd never seen him with her own eyes, she knew he was with her.

"Edward?" Maria said, her lips parting into a smile. "What did you make of Mrs. Fisher? Did you see her late husband?" Maria pushed her library book, *The Rescuers*, aside where a pen had been resting under it. She slid a piece of paper beneath her right hand. Then she balanced the pen between her knuckles over the paper. Very slowly, Edward's cool grip guided Maria's hand across the paper, allowing the pen to leave a most mysterious reply:

Mrs. Fisher may be foolish to believe her,
But her heart is far wiser and sweeter.

2
Dig Up the Dead

After ten minutes, the front door slammed. Heavy footsteps hammered the floor, until Maria snapped from her trance. The closet door flew open, flooding her room with light.

"John screwed up again," said Madame Destine. She brushed the parrot off her shoulder and pulled the fur coats across the bar with a harsh screech. She slipped out of her mink and slung it on Maria's mattress. The fringed dress Madame Destine wore might have once belonged to a flapper during the 1920s, but after a century, it was riddled with moth holes and stains.

Maria stood up. "Did she fall for it?" she asked.

"Too soon to tell," said Madame Destine.

"I did it as we rehearsed. When Mr. Fox started in on the pipes early, I turned on the fan, too."

"Yeah, yeah, yeah." Madame Destine shook her off

impatiently and threw on a black fur. She looked like a giant stain in the bright room. Houdini fluttered back to her shoulder. "That woman better come through. If she loved her husband, she'll do as she's told."

Maria thought about the old woman. Mrs. Fisher seemed kind, and she could tell the widow would do anything for her husband. Kindhearted people could be gullible. But something pulled at Maria. Edward had said her heart was wise and sweet. "But . . . ," began Maria, her voice wavering. "Do you feel like what we're doing is . . . wrong?"

Madame Destine stopped.

She turned around to face her child, her eyes narrowing as if to study her. "My sweet and caring Maria," she said. "Have I not told you again and again? There's no right and wrong, only—"

"Opportunity," they said in unison. Madame Destine shouted it with gusto, but Maria only mumbled it.

"OPPORTUNITY! OPPORTUNITY!" mimicked Houdini.

"Knock it off!" Madame Destine said. She held her parrot's beak in place, but he shook his head free and shifted farther down her arm.

Maria slipped past Madame Destine and into the light of her mother's master bedroom, where a queen-size bed and a dresser were surrounded by four walls decorated with yellowed newspaper clippings—all obituaries going back many years. The clippings had been tacked in clumps, one on top of the other, and a light breeze from the two open windows sent the papers fluttering.

"Besides," Madame Destine added, handing Maria a broom, "that old bag has no relatives. She'll take that ring to her grave, where someone else will snatch it. I'm just getting there first." Then she pointed to the kitchen. "Shouldn't you be cleaning—"

The door to the kitchen swung open, and a tall, thin man with dark features wearing a black turtleneck and a newsboy cap stepped in. His heavy unibrow stretched over his face. "Can't hear a stinkin' thing in the basement!" he said. "I bang on the pipes, I do my moaning, but I can't for the life of me hear my cues!"

Madame Destine greeted him with a stern look. "You came in too early, John."

"I'll do better next time," said Mr. Fox.

"Well, clean out your ears. You almost ruined it for us!"

Maria quickly added, "It's okay, Mr. Fox. I was able to turn on the fan. She didn't notice a thing."

John Fox rubbed his chin. Then he lifted his heavy brow. "Did she take the bait?"

Madame Destine's smile snaked across her face. "She took the bait. She'll likely investigate the organization to see if it's legit. Did you finish the website?"

"I worked all night on it," Mr. Fox answered. "I made it real nice, see?" He brought out his phone and typed something before he held it up.

Madame Destine slapped the phone out of his hand. "It's gotta match the business card! Who's gonna support an organization that doesn't look legit?"

"Aye-aye, Captain!" Mr. Fox said with a salute.

Maria tugged on Mr. Fox's sweater and dug into the pockets of her patched blue jeans. "If you want me to take a look, I can help like I did with the bait." Maria pulled a business card from her pocket that read

MR. BENJAMIN EDMOND FACTOR
Brooklyn Urban Youth Initiative for Tomorrow
Giving Children an Opportunity to Grow
718-555-5555
www.buyit.org

Mr. Fox slapped the card out of her hand. "I don't need no help from a kid!" he said. "You just go back in that closet and stay put."

"Mr. Fox!" exclaimed Maria, trying to keep her voice from shaking as she picked up one of her library books from her mother's dresser. "I can't be in two places at once! How can I be in my room when I have to clean in the kitchen?" Maria hugged the broom and book as she slid behind her mother.

Mr. Fox was unmoved. "I don't like your girl doing all this reading." His lips curled before turning his gaze on Maria. "She's gonna get too smart for her own good."

Maria gripped her book a little harder.

"Knock it off, John," said Madame Destine as she fluffed up her collar and straightened her turban. "My little girl's gonna have brains just like her mama. One day you'll be Madame Destine, Maria, just like your grandmama before me."

Maria tried to picture herself in her mother's heavy turban and musty coat, but she couldn't see it. Although a life of conning was all she'd ever known, Maria wondered if there was something better for her out there. Something that involved actually helping people—like the characters she'd read about in books.

Maria gazed up at the poster that read MADAME DESTINE, THE GREATEST SPIRITUALIST MEDIUM. The portrait of her grandmother under the banner showed a soft, saintly looking woman.

Madame Destine pushed Maria toward the kitchen door, but Maria kept her gaze on the portrait. She'd inherited her grandmother's large brown eyes and soft, round face. "Is it true that Grandma really did convene with the spirits?" she asked. "The papers say she was a real diviner."

Madame Destine moved slowly across the floorboards with her daughter. "Now, Maria," she said, pushing her through the kitchen door, "how many times have I told you? There's no such thing as spirits. People who think that stuff is real are foolish!" Madame Destine playfully jabbed Maria in the side with her elbow, but it hurt.

"FOOLISH! FOOLISH!" squawked Houdini.

"Knock it off!" Madame Destine shouted. Houdini turned around and fluffed his feathers.

"But what if—"

"I mean it, child! Your grandmother shared none of her secrets with me. I don't know her method, but take it from me: Hard work and crafty research is needed to dig up the dead. You can only see into the past by using the magic of your wits and natural instincts. Haven't you learned how to use the library?"

Maria put down the book and began sweeping the floor while her mother followed behind her. "Mom, I told you! I've BEEN using the library. I'm always reading stuff I like."

"Ah! Stories! It's a waste of time. You need facts. Facts for you to use to your advantage." Her lips slithered into a smile. "You should be researching public records and family trees, snipping obituaries and highlighting their survivors. We're researching widows, my dear. LONE. SURVIVING. WIDOWS."

"Okay," murmured Maria. She rested the broom against the counter and filled the sink with water.

"Good! And don't you forget it. Now, clean up the place while Mama's gone. Me and John are off to scrounge up some dinner." She slid her arm through Mr. Fox's, and the two of them exited the apartment through the front door, leaving Maria alone in the kitchen to ponder spirits and libraries, fiction and facts.

3
Edward

Maria scrubbed the stove with steel wool, her fingers stained with pink soap and grime. Her mother had been gone for a while, and she had already mopped the floor, but Maria didn't want to stop cleaning before she returned, or she'd be accused of slacking off.

She kept scrubbing until the back of her head tickled. Then her skin began to tingle. She loved this feeling. "I know you're here, Edward," she said to the empty kitchen with a smile. Her hands were grimy, but she didn't care. Edward had a way of making her feel special—as if she were Cinderella and her life of scrubbing and conning was only temporary.

She threw the steel wool into the sink and wiped off her hands. "Why don't you tell me about Mrs. Fisher and her late husband?" she said, smiling.

Maria pulled out a vinyl chair from the table. "I'm almost ready," she said.

What she loved most was hearing about the lives of the departed. She loved it almost as much as she enjoyed reading a good book. She'd been wondering about Mrs. Fisher's husband ever since the séance.

Maria slid out a piece of plain white paper from under the empty fruit bowl and placed it in front of her. Then she grabbed a pen and rested it lightly between her two knuckles over the paper. She shut her eyes, threw her head back, and cleared her mind. The faint water drops from the sink and the occasional honk outside shrank away from her consciousness.

Everything was still.

As it should be.

Suddenly, her hand pulled back. Then forward. Then this way and that—in quick swoops. The pen balanced between her knuckles, forming tiny flourishes of fine penmanship.

Then her hand stopped, and the pen rolled off her knuckles.

Maria awoke from her trance a little groggy, with the warmth returning to her fingers. She picked up the paper and gave it a read:

Poor, penniless Mrs. Fisher
Will miss the ring on her finger.
But hidden inside her flat,

Her fortune rests untapped.
Mr. Fisher hopes that you'll help her
Find what she will treasure.

Maria was puzzled by the message. Edward usually gave details about the dead that contradicted her mother's charade, but never a request.

Maria read the note again, allowing Mrs. Fisher's troubles to sink in. It was clear that the widow was broke. But so was Maria. Mrs. Fisher's late husband had asked that she help her find wealth hidden in her flat—her apartment. Edward knew Maria was forbidden to talk to anyone. Why was he asking her this favor now? But this was Edward, and she trusted him more than her mother. And maybe there was something in it for Maria—like treasure. Maria scrunched her brow. "Okay. Tell me where the fortune is, Edward."

Maria positioned the pen in place between her knuckles, closed her eyes again, and rested back in her chair. She waited for Edward to take hold of her hand.

And suddenly he did.

Maria's hand traveled the paper, back and forth, allowing the pen to make its mark. She could almost feel him reaching over her, as her hand lost all feeling from the cold that engulfed it.

WHAM!

The pen fell to the floor.

Maria opened her eyes. She heard footsteps down the hall. Her mother must have returned! Quickly, she read the message:

Tell her first:
Remember the light of the silvery moon
And the honeymoon a-shining in June.

What was this? Was she supposed to relay a cheesy love note to Mrs. Fisher from her late husband? She could get in a lot of trouble for contacting Mrs. Fisher.

The bickering of Mr. Fox and Madame Destine echoed down the hallway to the kitchen. Trying not to panic, Maria shoved the two sheets of paper under the fruit bowl. Then she picked up the mop and slid the soapy water across the floor.

Madame Destine entered with a plastic sack and slammed a jar of salsa on the counter. "Still at it?" she asked Maria before popping open the lid. "We're having chips and dip for dinner."

Mr. Fox entered the kitchen with a mouth full of tortilla chips, the crumbs stuck to the front of his turtleneck. Madame Destine glanced behind her at Mr. Fox. "Or just dip," she added.

Maria put the mop away. Then she turned on the stove and emptied the contents of the jar into the pot. Her stomach growled, but she refrained from taking a bite of the sauce before it cooked. She sprinkled salt and pepper onto the mushy substance while it hissed and popped against the pot. Maria made a disgusted face. Her last three meals had been chips and dip.

If only she could have a real meal.

They needed that ring from the widow or else she would starve. "When do you think she'll call?" Maria asked.

"Give it a day or two," stated Madame Destine in an absent voice, her eyes scanning the obituaries at the kitchen table.

Mr. Fox finished the chips and crinkled the bag. "Mark my words, she'll call tonight," he said. He dug in his pocket and pulled out his cell phone.

Maria removed three bowls from the cupboard and spooned two scoops of the hot dip into each bowl. She set the food on the table and said, "Dinner is served!"

The three sat at the table and shoveled the hot salsa into their mouths, staring at the silent phone with hungry eyes.

And like a strange omen, the phone rang, and the three of them jumped.

Mr. Fox lunged for the cell phone and fumbled with it before he was able to answer. "B-B-Brooklyn Urban Youth Initiative for Tomorrow! This is Benjamin speaking!" he declared in a professional voice that almost sounded intelligent to Maria. She was impressed and nodded to her mother.

Madame Destine looked directly at Mr. Fox and mouthed, *Is it her?*

Mr. Fox brought his thumb up and smiled. "Yes, we do accept donations, including jewelry . . . It's for the annual fund-raiser auction. Yes. In the past some of the jewelry has sold for a bundle and kept our organization going strong."

Madame Destine nodded, satisfied with the delivery of Mr. Fox's answers. Maria had heard them rehearsing the scheme ever since her mother had thought it up. Madame Destine nudged Maria and said under her breath, "If you wanna get anywhere in this world, don't have a bank account. Operate in jewels and cash only. Otherwise you leave a paper trail that can be followed."

Maria had no clue what her mother meant, but she knew the ring would soon be in their hands, just like the other times. There had been the psychic hotline until they got rid of the landline. Then there was the internet astrology scheme and the psychic life coach for bankers willing to make risky investments. And all of these schemes had filled her stomach with food.

But Edward had asked her to help Mrs. Fisher, a woman who was penniless just like them. She felt slightly guilty for having a small part in the con, yet why had Edward asked her to help THIS particular widow and not the other victims? Maria wanted to do the right thing; she really did. But would it be worth her starving? She decided to compromise. She would help Mrs. Fisher find her fortune, but only after they got her ring. It was a tactic she'd learned from her mother: *You scratch my back, I'll scratch yours.*

"So, you wanna think about it?" continued Mr. Fox. "Well, we would really appreciate the donation . . . Yes, the fund-raiser is soon . . . We're just getting the dates squared away . . . The sooner you drop off the donation, the better . . . Drop it by my office on Waverly like it says on the website . . . Right. By the garage in the alley . . . You want a day to think about it? Well, suit yourself."

Mr. Fox ended the call and hit the table with his fist. "She's not sold on it!"

"Not sold?" Madame Destine declared with astonishment. "This is my best plan yet!"

"She needs a day to think it over," said Mr. Fox, as he wiped his mouth with his sleeve. Then he threw his spoon in his bowl.

Madame Destine's face lost all color. In a whisper, she said, "You know what this means, don't you, Fox?" She pushed her bowl away and leaned toward him. "She's gonna do one of two things: investigate the organization or come back here looking for more proof that she really was talking with her husband!"

Mr. Fox's eyebrows bunched together. "You know anything else about her dead hubby?"

"Nothing!" Madame Destine's voice hammered.

The room was silent. Maria knew she must get the message to Mrs. Fisher, but when would she be able to talk to

her? Even if Mrs. Fisher returned to their apartment, there was a chance Maria would be at the library. Maria cleared her throat. "Why don't you let me talk to her?"

Madame Destine and Mr. Fox turned to Maria. For a moment, time stopped, lost in the frostbite of their eyes.

"Maybe talking to a child would soften her heart and make it easier to give her pledge?" Maria shrugged, but there was worry in her voice. She tried to act as if her suggestion was completely normal, but she knew it wasn't. Maria grew anxious and stood up from the table, clearing it and rushing over to the sink.

"What a load of bunk!" snapped Mr. Fox. "You see, Destine?" he said, rubbing his jaw. "She's getting too smart for her own good!"

Madame Destine narrowed her eyes and pulled out the two sheets of paper from under the fruit bowl. "What's this? 'Remember the light of the silvery moon, and the honeymoon a-shining in June.' Who's this to, Maria?"

Maria dropped one of the bowls, and it shattered on the floor.

She felt as if she was not inside her body. Maria frantically tried to come up with some excuse, but all she could think of was what her mother would do if she found out about Edward. Would she force her to con widows by pumping Edward for information about their dead relatives? Or would she think Maria had lost her mind and send her away? Maria didn't want to find out. "It's just some research

I was doing in the library," she said in a chipper tone. At that moment, Maria needed Edward with her. Just the cool tingling of his presence would be enough to comfort her.

"And what's this paper say?" asked Madame Destine. Her eyes scanned the second page. "This is about Mrs. Fisher . . . and her ring . . . and her fortune?"

"FORTUNE! FORTUNE!" squawked Houdini.

"That's right!" Madame Destine's smile was thin and sharp. She rubbed her parrot's head and sang, "Fortuuuuune!" Then she stopped and addressed Maria. "Whose handwriting is this? The librarian's?"

Mr. Fox peered over Madame Destine's shoulder and scratched at his head through his cap.

"Yes!" Maria said, a little out of breath while she swept up the shards of broken bowl. "It's just something she copied from a book and gave me. I was researching the Fisher family."

Madame Destine's smile fell flat, and a hard crease pulled her lip up to her nose. "Don't toy with me, child! What's this about a ring? Did you tell someone about our scheme?"

"Not at all! I talk to NO ONE, like you've told me," Maria said, trying to stay calm. "It's just a coincidence that a ring is mentioned in the passage."

Madame Destine's eyes pressed into Maria, but she said nothing. Instead, she folded the two papers into a tiny square and stuffed them into her fur coat. Then she slowly eased back in her chair while Houdini wobbled on her shoulders.

Maria felt the cool-air tingle of Edward's presence, and she felt safe again. She took a deep breath and straightened her posture. "If you'll excuse me, I think I'll go read in my room."

Neither Madame Destine nor Mr. Fox moved their lips to respond. Their unblinking eyes said it all, probing Maria for more.

Maria turned around and headed to her closet with all the confidence she could muster. But in the back of her mind, she wondered if she was walking away from a terrible accident.

4
A Restless Spirit

The next day, Maria hurried down the uneven sidewalk to the library. The one-story, modern structure was wedged between two four-story Victorian brownstones and reminded her of an adopted child standing between older parents. The library building, like her, was a misfit in its surroundings. But upon entering the two doors, she felt safe and welcome.

Although Maria had read all the books in the small children's section, she didn't mind revisiting them. After all, they'd been her lifelong friends.

Today she needed to cover her tracks and make it look like she'd been researching the Fishers. Mr. Fox and her mother were already suspicious. She'd spent a restless night in her closet worrying about her mother confiscating Edward's words. She was happy to escape the house for the library, which was the only place she was allowed to go.

Since Madame Destine homeschooled her, she *had* to let her daughter get books from *somewhere*.

Maria searched the obituaries, jotting down any notes. Then she sighed. What she wanted right now was to escape. Escape from her lonely life conning widows. She folded the paper and scanned the library. It was mostly strollers and nannies, but there was one kid there. It was the boy who had moved in upstairs from her—she knew because he was always wearing a red ball cap. He had a light brown complexion and a nice smile and appeared to be immersed in his book. Her mother had forbidden Maria from speaking to him.

Maria didn't own any books at home. She had no television, no music, no computer—no possessions of any kind; just plain, blank sheets of paper and a couple of pens. But in the library, for brief moments, she could read books and live other people's lives.

She'd read everything by Louis Sachar, Natalie Lloyd, and Sheila Turnage. She'd gone along with Cass and Max-Ernest on their adventures against the Midnight Sun in the Secret Series. She'd been there with Mary when she discovered the key to the door in *The Secret Garden*. And she'd helped Kyle solve the clues in the Lemoncello books.

Maria sank deep into her chair and blew the hair from her face. "How do I find her, Edward?" she said, half to herself and half to his spirit, who she hoped was somewhere nearby listening. "Where should I look for Mrs. Fisher?

If you're there, tell me what I should do." Maria glanced around to make sure no one was watching.

She saw Ms. Madigan, scarcely the size of a splinter and lit with red hair, shelving books. She seemed too busy to pay attention to what Maria was about to do. Maria closed her eyes and balanced the pen between her knuckles on top of the paper, then waited for the familiar tingle of Edward to take hold and guide her. She waited and waited until—

"Maria, what are you doing?"

Maria took a quick breath and slowly opened her eyes. There was no telling how many hours she'd been sitting there.

Ms. Madigan stood before her with a police officer in a black uniform. "We're closing soon," she said, "But I'd like you to speak to Officer O'Malley for a few minutes before you go."

A policeman? Here to see her? Maria darted her eyes around the library and realized that most of the visitors had left. She swallowed, trying not to think what would happen if her mother knew a cop wanted to ask her a few questions. That was her mother's golden rule: no talking to the police. But she had no choice. "Uh, okay," said Maria.

Officer O'Malley had a bushy brow with a wave of hair that swept above his forehead and splashed into his ears. He pulled out a chair next to Maria's and eased onto the edge of it, his knees nearly lifting the table in front of him. He leaned in and, in a sympathetic tone, asked, "Is . . . everything okay at home?"

Maria could tell by how delicately he asked the question that things definitely didn't appear okay to him. That Ms. Madigan! She'd tipped off the cop. The librarian seemed so innocent when she took the position there six months ago. First, she'd asked Maria how she enjoyed her books. Then she started suggesting some for her to read. Then the book club. Why was Ms. Madigan interfering with her home life? Maria knew that whatever she did, she must act normal. "Sure," she said, but it came out in more of a whimper.

Officer O'Malley's forehead creased before he leaned in closer to Maria. "Ms. Madigan tells me you're the star reader in her library club."

Maria eyed the book in front of her and brought it closer. She loved the library club, but she couldn't understand how it had gotten her into trouble with Ms. Madigan.

"She tells me you're here every day, unattended by a guardian," said Officer O'Malley.

"Mom homeschools me," Maria said quickly. "She trusts me to do my work without supervis—"

"I've been informed that she homeschools you," said the officer, cutting her off.

Ms. Madigan peeked from behind the officer, holding a stack of books as if she intended to shelve them, but she didn't move. Worry lines formed between her eyebrows.

"Ms. Madigan informed me she gave you a permission slip to have signed," said Officer O'Malley.

"A permission slip?" asked Maria, trying to sound innocent. She vaguely remembered throwing one away two weeks ago. Her mother didn't want her signature on anything.

"To be signed by your guardian, so you could have your picture taken next to your book report for the library newsletter." Officer O'Malley motioned with his eyes to the glass case by the entrance, where Maria's shadow box was prominently displayed. "Didn't you give it to her?"

"No," said Maria before looking down at the book in front of her. Whatever she did, she needed to get him off her. A snoop could land her mother in jail.

"You forgot to give her the form?" asked the officer.

"I don't like having my photo taken," Maria said, before adding, "I'm camera shy."

Officer O'Malley appeared to be thinking as he pursed his lips. "We tried calling your mother at the number on your library account, but it seems as if the phone has been disconnected."

"Mom got a cell phone," Maria said, making her voice firm to dismiss suspicion. "She disconnected the landline." Maria tilted her head to see behind the officer. Ms. Madigan appeared nervous, shifting the weight of the books to her other arm.

Officer O'Malley gave a long exhale before he said, "Can I have her new phone number?"

Maria knew she shouldn't give the officer her number. If

he called, he might discover the scam and arrest her mother, but if she did nothing, it would make him even more suspicious. He might even show up at her house.

With some hesitation, Maria reached into her pocket, ignoring the library card and loose change, and pulled out the business card she'd designed for Mr. Fox. "Here's her work number," said Maria, but before she handed it to him, she stopped. "Is there any reason to call her if I don't want my picture taken?" Maria tried to steady her hand from trembling.

Officer O'Malley glanced at Ms. Madigan before he shrugged. "No. I guess not."

Maria's heart pounded as she tried to take slow, steady breaths. She pulled the card away and stuffed it back into her pocket.

"Can I go now?" asked Maria.

"Yes, you're free to go," said Officer O'Malley.

Maria grabbed her book and took deliberate steps to the kiosk by the doors. She yanked out her library card from her pocket causing a few coins and something to fall out and hit the floor. Then she scanned her card before holding the book's barcode under the red light. The kiosk dinged, signaling that the book was checked out. Maria dashed to the entrance.

"You dropped something!" called Ms. Madigan, but Maria didn't care. She'd just escaped a sinking ship, and she wasn't going to be detained any longer. But as she went through the first door, she could feel the librarian and the cop watching her. Heart pounding, she pushed open the second door and took in a gulp of fresh air. She was free, just narrowly escaping drowning in a whirlpool of questions.

☀ ☀ ☀

A few days later, Maria picked her way over the jagged slabs of sidewalk pushed up by the trees lining her block. The brownstones glowed burgundy and orange as the sun melted into the tops of the buildings. The leaves crunched under her feet. Maria held her hand out and hit every iron bar on the ornate fences and gates guarding the apartments. When she reached her home, she noticed the curtains had been pulled and the neon PSYCHIC sign flickered and buzzed in the front window. This was her mother's signal that she was not to be disturbed.

Maria perched on the steps outside her building and opened one of her books. It was not the first time she'd had to wait outside. For a few seconds, she shut her eyes and listened to the other kids playing down the block. The wheels of a skateboard popped and grumbled against the grit of the pavement, and a ball bounced between shouts and laughter. The strollers rattled over the bumpy sidewalk like covered wagons, making their way to Fort Greene Park.

The autumn breeze blew around her as she cradled her book, running her fingers across the embossed title: *From the Mixed-Up Files of Mrs. Basil E. Frankweiler.*

Whhhack!

Maria's head knocked back. Stunned, she opened her eyes to find a red rubber ball rolling under her feet.

"My bad! My bad!" called a voice. The slap of feet moved toward her. "I'm really sorry! Are you okay?"

Maria shook her head before she could focus on who was standing on the other side of the gate. "I'm not okay. Your ball hit me."

"I'm really sorry," said the boy from the library, adjusting his ball cap. "I'm not so good at throwing, but you probably guessed that."

Maria rubbed her head. "Well, it looks like you hit your target."

He laughed. "I wasn't aiming for you. I didn't take into account the wind! It was supposed to go over there." The boy pointed down the block at a group of kids. He turned and grinned.

He had a gap between his front teeth that made a pleasant smile.

"I'm Sebastian," he said. "Who are you?"

"I'm Maria."

"What grade are you in?" asked Sebastian. "I'm in fifth. But was bumped up a year." He pushed his glasses up his nose and waited for Maria to answer.

"Grade level doesn't interest me," Maria said with a shrug.

"So . . . is it true?" Sebastian asked, with a nervous crack in his voice. "Are you the girl that lives with the psychic?"

Maria knew she was not supposed to answer questions from anyone. If her mother saw her talking to this boy, she would yell. But before she knew it, she found herself blurting, "Sure, I guess. She's just my mom."

"We moved in above you last month. I see you at the library, but you never play outside. How come?"

More questions? She should shut her mouth, but she wanted him to stay just a little longer. She shrugged. "I got things to do."

"What kinds of things?" asked Sebastian. "Psychic things?"

Maria rolled her eyes. If only he knew the half of it. But she was keeping her mouth shut.

"And why is the super always in your apartment?" asked Sebastian. "Mr. Fox doesn't fix a thing in ours."

Sebastian had gone too far with his questions. Maria had to end the conversation before it went any further. "You ask too many questions," she told him, turning back to her book and opening it.

Sebastian looked down and kicked at a crooked slab of sidewalk. Maria peeked at him from the corner of her eye.

"You wanna play ball?" he finally asked.

Maria shook her head, staring down at her book. "I can't today," she mumbled, but she knew she was forbidden to ever play with other kids. Her mother didn't want anyone snooping in their business.

The kids down the street called out for Sebastian. He cleared his throat and asked, "Can you hand me the ball?"

Maria retrieved the ball from the step and threw it to Sebastian, but he missed. "I guess I'm not so good at catching!" he said, trying to shake it off with a laugh, but Maria could tell he was embarrassed.

"Sports aren't really my thing either." Maria smiled just a little, but inside she was hurting.

Sebastian retrieved the ball and gave his gap-toothed grin.

Maria turned around to see if her mother was looking. The window was dark and foreboding, the heavy curtains still drawn. She wanted to be with the other kids—laughing and playing ball.

Sebastian lingered a moment, tossing the ball in the air.

Maria shut her eyes, still facing her apartment. *Please go away*, she thought. After a few moments, she heard Sebastian's feet slap the sidewalk as he ran back down the block to join the other kids.

Maria opened her eyes. The other kids had forgotten her and had begun their game again. She studied her book, but no longer felt like reading.

The door to her apartment swung open, startling Maria into dropping her book. A middle-aged man exited her home. Madame Destine pulled the curtains and peered through the rippled glass at Maria. Then the buzzing of the neon sign died, and its soft glow faded to darkness.

5
A Return Client

The next morning, Maria drew the heavy curtains in the front parlor, allowing the light from outside to beam through the stuffy room. Tiny particles of dust floated around her like snow, settling over a card table with a paisley tablecloth splattered with candle wax. The dust drifted to the two folding chairs and onto Houdini's cage, which was covered with seeds, feathers, and bird droppings.

Maria wondered why her mother never cleaned the birdcage herself. He was HER parrot, after all.

She took out Houdini from the cage and patted his feathers before feeding him a few seeds. "It'll only be a minute. You'll have your cage back in no time," she said, placing him on top of his stand. She poured dish soap into a bucket of water, dipped a rag in, and scraped away at the rusty cage.

Maria worked quickly, the suds wrinkling her fingers. Then she threw the rag into the bucket, picked up a broom, and swept away the seeds that had spilled from the cage.

She listened for the sound of her mother and Mr. Fox at the other end of the apartment.

Ka-thud!

Ka-thud!

Ka-thud!

Someone must be kicking a ball outside the building, she thought.

Maria dropped her broom and peered out the parlor window. Behind the ripple of glass stood a boy, his face hidden in the shade of his red ball cap. Maria squinted.

Sebastian?

Yes, it was Sebastian kicking a ball against the steps. Maria ducked behind the birdcage and peered between the vertical bars. The ball bounced rhythmically back and forth with every kick. Sebastian must have seen her looking, because he stopped and waved.

It was almost as if he was taunting her. Or maybe he was trying to get her attention, trying to say hello.

The front gate swung open, and Sebastian moved aside, his ball rolling beside the steps.

Wavering before him like a lily in the wind was the widow, Mrs. Fisher. She smiled warmly at the boy and scooted past him, making her way to the front door.

Maria snapped from her trance.

Buzzzz! Buzzzzz!

The widow had returned to speak to her late husband! Maria dragged the bucket and broom into the kitchen as fast as she could, while the buzzer rang through the apartment. Her feet slid against the wooden floorboards, her body crashing to the mattress in the closet.

Buzzzz! Buzzzz!

Maria slammed her door and pressed her eye against the hole in the wall.

Footsteps tapped across the apartment to the front parlor.

Madame Destine swung open the door. "What is it!" she barked, but then stopped. "I mean—er—welcome, dear friend!"

"Madame Destine!" said Mrs. Fisher. "I've been thinking about my late husband's request."

Madame Destine folded her arms and leaned against the door. "Go on . . ." Houdini mimicked her order.

"And if you're willing, I would like to make contact with him one more time."

Madame Destine gave a dramatic bow and steadied her turban. "Well, I've been expecting you," she said slowly. "Come inside, and I'll summon his spirit."

Mrs. Fisher tiptoed in and closed the door behind her.

Madame Destine yanked the curtains shut before she killed the lights. A match was struck and the two women were illuminated by soft candlelight. Madame Destine backed away from the table until she covered Maria's vent with her bottom.

Knock. Knock. Knock.

This was Madame Destine's signal for Maria to get ready.

"Mr. Fisher is nearby," began Madame Destine. "I can *feel* him in this very room," she continued in a whisper. "Come and sit with me at the table." She grabbed Mrs. Fisher by the hand and swung her in front of the card table.

Mrs. Fisher fell into her chair while Houdini was placed in his cage.

Madame Destine clapped her hands and held them high above her head. "Silence! I need absolute silence as I attempt to summon the dead."

Mrs. Fisher shut her eyes and sat motionless in her chair. The room was deathly silent.

Madame Destine began, "Spirit of the late Robert Fisher, I summon you to this table on behalf of your wife wishing to speak with you ONE. LAST. TIME."

Behind the wall, Maria felt the familiar frosty chill of Edward against the back of her neck. "Not now!" she whispered. "I have to work!" She waved her hand behind her while she peered through the grate.

She waited for Mr. Fox's moans and clanging pipes from the basement and quickly turned on the fan.

But once she'd ducked away from the fan, the cool air continued to whip around her face.

"Edward! Can't you see I'm busy?" she whispered. Maria felt around the floor for a pen and paper.

Ka-thud!

Maria stopped.

That must have been her mother's head hitting the table. She reached for the fan and turned it off. Then she grabbed the pen and placed it between her knuckles against the paper.

"Okay," she said out of breath. "Tell me. And hurry!"

Edward instantly took over, moving Maria's hand across the paper. When she stopped and the pen fell to the paper, Maria opened her eyes and scanned the note:

Marilyn will give your mother
The prize that she is after.
Then follow the widow home
And tell her alone what I told you.

Maria crumpled the note.

Oh, Edward! Why was he asking her to follow this stranger home? Didn't he know she could never get away long enough without arousing suspicion from her mother?

But she'd promised Edward she'd help him. She knew that helping the widow was the right thing to do. But why couldn't it be a simple task? One that wouldn't get her into trouble?

"Okay, Edward," she whispered. "I'll . . . I'll try." But Maria was not so sure of herself.

Madame Destine's voice boomed in the next room. "Goodbye, my love! I look forward to our reunion in the next world!" Her bracelets jangled, the pipes clanged, and the moans sang through the apartment. Maria switched on the fan until she heard the thud on the table and turned it off again. Then she peered through the vent.

Mrs. Fisher dug through her purse and handed Madame Destine a twenty-dollar bill. The fake psychic tucked the money into her bosom and tore open the curtains. Houdini fluttered back to her shoulder.

The widow eased out of her chair and drifted to the front door. "Thanks again," she said, taking Madame Destine's hand with a bow. "Now, the Brooklyn Urban Youth Initiative for Tomorrow is on Waverly and Atlantic? Which way is that?"

Madame Destine released her hand from the widow's grasp. "Take a left, and you'll walk straight to it." Madame Destine flung open the door and gave Mrs. Fisher a tap on the back, propelling her outside. She let the door slam behind her.

Maria backed away from the vent and threw on her hoodie. She had to follow Mrs. Fisher and do it fast! She took a deep breath and whispered, "Edward, you owe me."

Then she kicked open her closet door and raced through

her mother's bedroom, gliding across the hall to the front parlor.

Madame Destine's thin body charged for Maria. "Just where do you think you're going?"

Maria clenched her fists. "I forgot my library books. I'll be back soon!" she said. She sped full throttle at her mother, causing the fake psychic to spin and lose her balance as she passed.

"No running in this house!" barked Madame Destine, her turban falling over her eyes. She swept her hands about the room for her daughter like a lobster's claws in a tank.

Maria flew through the front door faster than Houdini could mimic "NO RUNNING!" She turned and ran as fast as her legs could carry her, passing the kids at play on the sidewalk.

"Hey, where are you going?" called Sebastian, running after her.

But Maria ignored him. She had no time to stop anyway.

She scanned the sidewalk for the widow until she spotted the familiar sway of Mrs. Fisher and her cape blowing in the wind.

WEST 4th STREET
WASHINGTON SQ

6
Ghosting the Widow

Maria's Converse sneakers hopped over the uneven sidewalk, dodging broken glass and sloppy spills. She stopped running to catch her breath. She'd made it to Atlantic Avenue, the edge of her neighborhood, where heavy traffic rumbled and honked. She'd never been much farther than this before.

After she caught her breath, she searched down the street for the familiar cape of Mrs. Fisher.

The woman couldn't have disappeared into thin air, she thought, as the slap of feet that had been following her slowed down. Maria swung around to discover Sebastian.

"Where are you running to?" he asked, wiping the sweat from his brow.

"Are you following me?" Maria knew she sounded harsh, but she was on a mission, and this kid was getting in the way. She turned and scanned the sidewalk again for the widow.

And then she saw her.

She was standing in front of a grimy building across the street. The old woman paused to look at the back of the business card and held it up to the numbers over the unmarked door. Mrs. Fisher rang the buzzer to the foreboding building while a truck unloaded boxes into the garage next door.

"Why are you hanging out by Atlantic?" asked Sebastian. "There's nothing over—"

"Shhh!" said Maria, pushing him behind her. "You'll mess it up."

Mrs. Fisher tried knocking on the door this time. After a long pause, she stepped away from the door and turned around.

Maria stopped and watched the widow.

Mrs. Fisher twisted her wedding band around her finger and began to walk away from the building.

"Hey, missus. You looking for something?" called a voice from the garage.

Mrs. Fisher stopped.

There, from the shadows of the alley, stepped Mr. Fox. He was sweating under a suit that was too small for him. A bolo tie dangled from his neck. The strings were joined unevenly by the turquoise clasp, as if it were a noose.

"Why, yes." Mrs. Fisher's voice wavered. "I'm looking for the Brooklyn Urban Youth Initi—"

"You got the right place, lady," said Mr. Fox. "You the one that called the other day?"

Mrs. Fisher frowned and brought her hand up to her chest. "Why, er—yes. That was me, but is *this* a nonprofit?"

"Yeah, what's it to ya?"

Mrs. Fisher shook her head and backed away, but Mr. Fox swooped in front of her, pushing her shoulder toward the building. "Relax, lady. This is our loading dock, where we receive deliveries. The kiddies are down the block!"

Mrs. Fisher seemed to be relieved, bringing her hand up to her head to flatten her hair. "Okay! I was beginning to think that this place was—"

"The place is legit, lady," Mr. Fox assured her, and gave her a fake smile. "Didn't you have a donation for our charity?" He opened the door to the building and pushed the lady inside.

Maria could feel Sebastian watching her. She turned around.

"Are you spying on that lady?" asked Sebastian. The traffic at the end of the block almost drowned out his voice.

"Of course not!" Maria found some scraps of old newspaper in the trash by the curb. She grabbed one for herself and shoved the other into Sebastian's hands. "Quick.

Make yourself look busy!" Then she hid her face behind the newsprint.

"You ARE spying!" Sebastian said, before hiding behind his paper, too. They said nothing for four whole seconds before Sebastian peeked above the newsprint. "Why are we following her?" he whispered.

"Sebastian, please leave!"

Sebastian dropped the paper. "Okay. I get the message. I just wanted to see what you spend all your time doing!" He turned around and disappeared down the block.

A moving van pulled away from the garage, and behind it stood a bewildered Mrs. Fisher. She stepped past the driveway, shaking her head.

But the ring was missing from her finger!

Maria brought the paper up to her face as the widow shuffled past her. She waited until Mrs. Fisher had hiked half a block before she followed.

The old woman quickly turned the corner onto Fulton Street, where there was a cluster of restaurants. Maria weaved through the pedestrians with baby carriages until Mrs. Fisher descended the stairs into the subway.

But Maria stopped at the entrance.

She'd never left her neighborhood, much less ridden a train. What if she got lost and couldn't find her way back? Maria began to shake and took a deep breath to calm herself. There was no time for worry.

Soon Mrs. Fisher would be gone forever. Maria willed herself forward and descended the stairs to the C train, the temperature dropping as she fell into the shadows of the station.

The widow fumbled through her purse until she pulled out a MetroCard and swiped it through the turnstile. Maria didn't have a MetroCard or any money to buy one, but she knew she couldn't turn back. She'd promised Edward.

Mrs. Fisher passed through the turnstile.

Maria waited for the widow to descend the second set of stairs that led to the train before she approached the entrance.

The turnstile came up to her chest. It would be so easy to hop over it. Maria looked around. The station was empty.

"DO IT," she told herself.

She knew she was taking a risk, and she was not a risk taker.

Maria took a deep breath. She slapped the metal turnstile with both hands and lifted her legs high above it. Then she flung her body over and landed on her feet. Maria steadied herself and took off after the widow.

The train entered the station just as Maria was descending the stairs. She hopped aboard and exhaled, blowing the hair out of her face. Maria grabbed hold of the pole while the train rocked back and forth and increased in speed. This was her first time on a train, and a mixture of excitement and fear overcame her. It felt so good to be moving somewhere fast, to be anyplace but her stuffy closet at home. Maria scanned the seated passengers for Mrs. Fisher's plaid cape and her bright white hair.

There was a white hoodie on a teenager, a plaid sweater on an old man, and a red ball cap on someone reading the paper. Then she spotted the widow. Mrs. Fisher was inspecting her wrinkled hand, rubbing her finger where the ring had rested for all those years.

In between the moments of exhilaration, Maria felt sorry for Mrs. Fisher and a little ashamed at having a part in the con. She hoped she would be able to make it up to her when she found the treasure in her apartment. But she had not anticipated the widow living this far away.

The train made many stops: first stopping at Lafayette, then Hoyt, then Jay Street, then High Street where it continued under the East River into Manhattan. Maria didn't sit down. She wanted to keep her eye on the widow.

At West Fourth Street, the train filled with more people. Maria glanced back at Mrs. Fisher's seat.

The widow was suddenly gone!

Maria dove for the door just before it closed, and landed on the platform.

People swirled around her, bumping into her as they exited the station. Students plugged into their headphones glided by. Tourists holding bags paused to look at a map. A blind man breezed past her, the sound of his tapping cane becoming lost in the hollow thuds of beating bongos.

Maria pushed her way through the crowd gathered round the bongo player. She scanned the ramp of the exit, where she could just make out the familiar white hair of the widow weaving through a pack of people holding bags.

She chased after Mrs. Fisher, dodging a tattooed person with pink hair and just missing a family of tourists wearing I LOVE NY sweatshirts. She climbed the stairs into the gray light of the October sky.

Maria caught her breath, shaken by the heavy rumble of the trains below her.

Screeeeeeeech! A bus slowed down in front of her.

Honk! Honk! Honk! Honk! Taxis swerved around the bus letting off passengers.

Manhattan was much louder than the quiet library and peaceful sidewalks of her neighborhood in Brooklyn. And there were so many people. Maria waited behind Mrs. Fisher at the crosswalk, the yells from the crowd behind her soaring as a basketball hit a net. She spotted a movie theater across the street with a line outside it. The crosswalk sign turned white, and the mass of people walked down Sixth Avenue.

Like a swan caught in the rapids of a moving river, Mrs. Fisher's hair bobbed between the uneven lumps of heads in front of Maria. The old lady veered left down a tiny, quiet street that made a semicircle. She stopped in front of a brick town house with paint chipping off the door and dug through her purse for her keys.

Maria cleared her throat and pulled on Mrs. Fisher's cape. "Excuse me. Mrs. Fisher?"

The widow slowly turned around, a little startled. "Yes?" she said.

"I—I—I have a message for you."

"Oh? From whom?" asked Mrs. Fisher, a faint smile hinting at the corners of her lips.

"It's from your late husband." Maria tried to sound reassuring. "Can I talk—"

"What?" Mrs. Fisher stepped back, her expression troubled. "I'm sorry?"

"Please don't be angry with me," said Maria. "I was sent to—"

"My husband?" said Mrs. Fisher. She composed herself so that she stood just a little taller than Maria. "Who are you, and how do you know—"

"Robert Fisher has asked me to contact you," Maria said, and moved closer to Mrs. Fisher. Then she whispered, "He said I should tell you first: Remember the light of the silvery moon, and the honeymoon a-shining in June."

Mrs. Fisher slowly raised her hand to her heart. "Oh, good Lord," she whispered, and seemed to shrink.

"I didn't mean to disturb you," Maria added, and backed away. "He asked me to help you."

"Well, I, well, I . . ." Mrs. Fisher stuttered, and her words seemed to float higher and trail away from her. She straightened her glasses and examined Maria. After a long pause, she asked, "What's your name?"

"I'm Maria."

The widow nodded and said, "Would you like to come in for tea, Maria?"

Maria nodded.

Mrs. Fisher pulled out her keys and fumbled with the lock until it clicked.

The door slowly creaked open, and the two of them entered the widow's home.

7
A Vanished Era

Maria squinted into the dark hallway of Mrs. Fisher's apartment. She breathed in the musty air of dust and mothballs and the scent of flowery perfume and talcum powder. Maria held her nose. She'd stay five minutes, long enough to tell the widow the clue and find the treasure.

Mrs. Fisher's light steps shuffled past her down the hall. Then the lights flicked on.

Maria blinked.

There was so much stuff! From floor to ceiling, Mrs. Fisher's apartment was crammed with paintings, photographs, framed memorabilia, statues, masks, knick-knacks, and books.

The walls in Maria's home seemed dead with obituaries compared to Mrs. Fisher's walls, which were filled with life—*her* life.

A black cat darted behind the doorway to the bathroom, kicking kitty litter into the hallway.

A color photo hung by the door. It was a young woman wearing a turtleneck, embraced by a short, balding man wearing glasses. In another photo, the same pair was seated at a table with a group of adults laughing in a cafe.

This must be Mr. and Mrs. Fisher, thought Maria.

Maria couldn't believe how lovely and carefree Mrs. Fisher looked in the photo with her short, blond, wavy hair. There was another picture of a picnic with Mrs. Fisher wearing a crown of flowers and toasting a group of adults dressed in funny costumes.

A painting of a blue man with four arms smiled at Maria in the hallway. "That's my Shiva!" sang Mrs. Fisher. "He looks after the place while I'm gone. Have a seat on the sofa!" The old widow's heels tapped down the hall.

Maria paused to consider leaving again. If she sat on the couch, the widow would talk her ear off. She seemed lonely. But Maria had promised Edward she'd help.

She brushed her fingers against the contours of framed photos, arrowheads, and a Grecian vase. Maria crept to the glow of the living room.

The space was bright and flooded with light from two large windows. An upright piano stood against the wall with stacks of sheet music on the bench and the floor. *The widow must be a musician,* Maria thought.

She felt eyes staring down at her and swung around to

take in a wall of strange faces in all shapes and sizes. Maria caught her breath. She examined the beads and feathers hanging from the faces and thought they must be some kind of tribal masks, like the ones she'd seen in books.

Hung between the masks were more photos and paintings. At the far end of the room stretched a nine-foot dining room table covered in books, which seemed to make the space also a dining room. It was clear Mrs. Fisher was a reader. Maria exhaled at the sight of the books, feeling a little more comfortable in her surroundings.

Just as Maria eased onto the sofa, Mrs. Fisher entered the room with a tray containing a long, skinny loaf of bread and a dish of butter. She placed it on the chest that also served as a coffee table. "Voila! Here's a baguette," said Mrs. Fisher. "If you're hungry, then just help yourself. It's been so long since I've had a visitor. I wish I had more food!" A whistle blew in the other room. "Tea's ready!" The widow disappeared down the hallway again.

Maria hesitated before the food. If she ate it, she'd have to stay even longer than she'd planned.

Her stomach growled.

She knew she shouldn't take food from a stranger, but she tore off a small chunk of the baguette and spread some butter on it. Her teeth sank into the hard crust to discover soft bread in the center. It was so different than her usual snacks of beef jerky and Ding Dongs. Before she knew it, she'd eaten it.

Maria tore off another chunk from the baguette and

took a bite. Then she took another, and another. The bread was delicious.

Tiny squeaks grew louder in the hallway until Mrs. Fisher entered with a rolling cart. On it were two cups and saucers and a china teapot. The widow poured Maria a cup of tea. Then she opened a cupboard, thumbing through a bunch of cardboard sleeves. She pulled out a black disk from one sleeve and placed it carefully onto a box with knobs. She swung a small arm with a needle around and placed it on top of the disk.

"Have you ever seen one of these?" she asked.

"No. What is it?" Maria mumbled, covering her mouth since it was full.

"It's a record player."

The record scratched and skipped before the bongos and the deep pluck of melody from an upright bass became a song. Then a voice slipped lightly between the strings. "Place park, scene dark, silvery moon is shining through the trees." The voice was quirky, not at all perfect, but soft as a light breeze.

"This version is better than the Doris Day version of the time. The jazz clubs didn't want the girl next door to sing it." Mrs. Fisher smiled and sipped her tea.

"To my honey I'll croon love's tune. Honeymoon (honeymoon, honeymoon), Keep a-shining in June," chirped the voice under a low bass and drums.

"Only, I really was the girl next door. I was a Brooklyn

girl, just nineteen! It was about . . . 1959, and oh, New York was an exciting place!"

Then Maria knew it. This was Mrs. Fisher singing! Maria tried to do the math. How many years must have passed? It was another era. Another century. Wow! Mrs. Fisher was old!

"My father discovered I was singing after reading a review in the paper," Mrs. Fisher continued. "Boy, was he angry." She reached for the teapot and poured herself another cup. Then she offered more to Maria.

"But having the spotlight on you, staring out into the dark heads, the band behind me, and the microphone at my grasp—my voice in my ears—nothing else mattered." She closed her eyes and smiled while reaching for an invisible microphone. "And when I sang, ah . . . I was transported to another world!"

Maria set down her teacup. The widow needed to get to the point. "So, the message I gave you was a . . . a song that you sang?"

"It was our song," Mrs. Fisher said before opening her eyes again. "My husband was a regular at the Vanguard before we were married. If I didn't sing it, he would always request 'By the Light of the Silvery Moon.'" Mrs. Fisher lowered her voice. "It got to the point where I would sing it just for him—no one else in the club mattered. And one night he asked me out." Mrs. Fisher swung her tea up to her mouth and took another sip.

"And then . . . you got married?" asked Maria.

"After a little while we did, yes." Mrs. Fisher nodded. "Once he'd saved enough money to buy this apartment and fix it up. That's the only reason I'm not priced out of this neighborhood. Robby had the good sense to buy. This place had been a speakeasy where people drank during prohibition. But he sealed up all the escape routes used to fool the police when we moved in." Mrs. Fisher poured another cup of tea. "I knew when you told me those lines . . . you really had spoken with Robert. How could anyone know this? It was years ago!" Mrs. Fisher took a sip and set the cup down. "Now, enough about me. Who are you, and do I know your parents?"

Maria needed to tell Mrs. Fisher why she'd come. She wasn't here to talk about her family or hear about Mrs. Fisher's love life with her late husband. She'd come to find the widow's fortune. She'd hoped the lines would lead them somewhere. Maria tore off another piece of bread and chewed.

Coo-coo! Coo-coo!

A wooden bird shot its head out of a door beneath the shingled roof of the cuckoo clock, before retreating back inside. It was five o'clock. Maria knew she needed to get back. Her mother was probably angry and wondering where she was. But she hadn't told Mrs. Fisher why she'd come. Maria took a deep breath and decided to just come out and say it.

"Mr. Fisher has asked me to help you find a treasure hidden inside your apartment," Maria continued with her mouth full, no longer worried about her manners.

Mrs. Fisher was quiet for a long time. Finally, she said, "Treasure?" She shook her head. "I'm not sure there's anything of value in my home." Mrs. Fisher glanced at her finger where the ring once rested and frowned. "So . . . Maria, how did you come by this message from Robert? Did your parents put you up to this?"

"It's hidden here!" exclaimed Maria. "All I know is that I was asked to follow you here, give you the lines to the song, and help you find it."

Mrs. Fisher laughed. "The strange forces that bring people together!" She clapped her hands. Then her face grew serious. "Just how did Robert find you? Are you a psychic?" Mrs. Fisher gave a smirk.

"Well, he didn't actually *find* me," Maria said.

"Oh?" Mrs. Fisher met Maria's eyes, making her uncomfortable. Maria looked away.

Now what? Maria thought, chewing more slowly to buy herself some time before answering. She couldn't mention Edward. Finally, she swallowed and said, "Someone close to me talked to him." Maria had never told a living soul about Edward, and she wasn't about to tell a stranger.

"Does this someone talk to Robert regularly?" asked Mrs. Fisher.

Maria looked down at her feet.

Mrs. Fisher cleared her throat and said sharply, "Do I know your family?" She took off her glasses and began to polish them with the hem of her skirt.

Maria carefully ignored her question. "My friend talks to all kinds of . . . spirits," she replied, "but never with Mr. Fisher. And he never asks me to approach anyone. You're the first." Maria took a quick sip of tea. She hoped Mrs. Fisher wouldn't guess that her friend was a ghost!

"And this friend"—Mrs. Fisher paused deliberately— "tells you only what he hears from spirits?" She put on her glasses again and looked straight at Maria.

"He usually just gives me advice and comforts me when I'm sad." Maria took another bite of bread so that she wouldn't say too much.

She recalled Edward's sporadic visits. He'd tell her what the deceased relatives were really like. When Maria was sad, he'd pay her compliments, telling her how smart and pretty she was. And always there was his promise that things would change; her life would one day improve. After Maria finished chewing, she added, "He's my best friend."

"Well, it appears that your best friend has some kind of a gift. IF he can talk to spirits." Mrs. Fisher didn't sound convinced. "You must tell him to use his gift to make the world a better place." Mrs. Fisher paused and in a barely audible voice said, "And never let anyone tell him to stop."

Maria sensed the pain in her voice. "Why would my friend want to stop?" she asked.

Mrs. Fisher cleared her throat and said, "I imagine that a . . . *boy* talking to spirits is a hard thing for people to accept."

Maria's forehead wrinkled. She couldn't tell what Mrs. Fisher meant by that.

"Do your friend's parents know about this?" asked Mrs. Fisher.

Maria thought for a moment about Edward and realized she didn't know how old he was or even if his parents were still alive. Somehow, she'd always thought of him as older. She gave a quick shrug.

Mrs. Fisher raised her brow. "Each of us carries a gift inside us," she said. "Mine was singing. Could yours be telling stories?"

Maria shook her head. Where was Mrs. Fisher going with this?

"But my family didn't approve of my gift. After marriage, I took on a more traditional role . . . as just a wife."

"Why?" asked Maria. "I don't get it."

Mrs. Fisher laughed. "It was different times! In the 1960s that was just what women did: tend to their husbands."

"So . . . you gave up singing when you married Mr. Fisher?" Maria asked. She didn't understand why Mrs. Fisher was telling her this.

"Yes, he needed someone to help him with his dreams, so I gave up on mine. Now I deeply regret it. If your friend really can communicate with the dead, there will be opposition. Just like if you were, say, a storyteller, and strung together a tall tale after learning a few facts about an old woman somewhere . . ."

What? thought Maria. Was Mrs. Fisher accusing her of lying? After all she'd done? First escaping her mother, then hopping a turnstile—all to deliver Edward's message. Only to be called a liar?

"Perhaps if you used your stories in—"

Maria shot up from the sofa and blurted out, "Well, they're not made-up stories! And if you want your treasure, I guess you'll have to find it yourself." The clock was already at five thirty. It was time to go.

Maria placed the saucer and cup down on the trunk beside the sofa.

Mrs. Fisher reached out to stop Maria. "I didn't mean to upset—"

But Maria brushed past her.

"If you hear anything about Robert again, please do pay me another visit!" Mrs. Fisher called after her.

Maria shook her head. She knew the widow didn't believe her. Why would she ever come back?

Maria stomped down the hallway, nearly knocking over a Grecian vase. She tore past photos of Mr. and Mrs. Fisher by a pyramid, in a gondola, and on an elephant.

"Oh! Before you go," Mrs. Fisher called out from the living room. She shuffled down the hallway and grabbed her purse by the door. Then she dug through it.

Maria stopped, her hand on the knob, ready to fling open the door.

Mrs. Fisher pulled out her MetroCard and handed it to Maria. "This is to get you home safely." Mrs. Fisher lifted a brow. "I don't want you hopping any more turnstiles." Then her face softened to a smile. "Maybe I'll see you again?"

Maria snatched the card and murmured, "Thank you."

She couldn't help but wonder if Mrs. Fisher had known all along that she was being followed.

It didn't matter. She let the door shut behind her and stormed down the stairs. Then she tucked the MetroCard into her pocket and took one last glance up the stairs leading to Mrs. Fisher's apartment. She sensed she was leaving something strange and wonderful behind.

Maria turned around and discovered Sebastian waiting for her.

8
Two Rings

Why did you follow me again?" asked Maria. "I told you to go away!"

"I was making sure you were all right!" Sebastian said. "First I find you waiting in a dangerous alley. Then you hop a turnstile. Then you go into this stranger's house and disappear for an hour. I was seriously thinking of getting help."

"Well, now you see I'm okay," said Maria, folding her arms. "I don't need your help."

"Well, that's where you're wrong," said Sebastian, flashing his gap-toothed grin. "You need someone like me."

"Oh?" said Maria. She gave a fake laugh. "You mean like a sidekick?"

"Sure," said Sebastian, patting Maria's back, guiding her away from Mrs. Fisher's building. "The way I see it, everyone needs a friend."

Maria didn't like the sound of this. Sebastian could get her into a lot of trouble at home. They weaved through the hustle of students and street vendors as they turned onto Sixth Avenue. "I prefer to be alone," said Maria before stopping by a vendor with books laid out on a flattened cardboard box. It was true that books were her only friends, but something deep inside her told her to give Sebastian a chance. She thumbed through novels by Jack Kerouac, Paul Bowles, and Lawrence Ferlinghetti, but didn't recognize any of their names. Next to the books were stacks of used records. She searched for Mrs. Fisher's album in the pile but could feel Sebastian hovering near her.

"Well, are you going to tell me who she was?" asked Sebastian.

Maria looked up. "Who?"

"The old lady you followed home!" Sebastian crouched down beside her and began thumbing through records, too. "Who was she?"

Maria thought about ignoring him, but a burning question still lingered after she'd left Mrs. Fisher's apartment. Why would Edward lure her to the widow's home to find buried treasure but not tell her how to find it? Could he be playing a cruel joke on her? It didn't seem like Edward.

"Do you think people still bury treasures?" said Maria. "Today? In this city?" She knew that she was being a little cryptic, but for all practical purposes, Sebastian was as much a stranger to her as Mrs. Fisher.

"What do you mean?" Sebastian asked. "Like pirate's treasure?"

"Sure. I guess," said Maria. She didn't recognize any of the records.

"Probably not pirate's gold, but my dad tells me some of his clients have secret rooms in their apartments to hide with their valuables in case of a break-in. Does that count?" The two began to walk toward the train together. "Does this have something to do with the lady you visited?" he asked.

Maria shrugged. "I don't know. Have you ever had someone play a mean trick on you?"

Sebastian paused for a minute while they descended the stairs. Maria swiped her card through the turnstile, and Sebastian did the same. "Sure," he said, before catching up with her on the slanted walkway to the Brooklyn tracks. "Once when I used to play soccer, my team decided to completely ignore me. You know, because I'm no good."

Maria remembered how bad Sebastian was at throwing and catching, so she nodded.

"One day, I got an invitation to a birthday party by one of the players on the team. I was so excited because I really wanted the team to like me. When my mom took me to Chuck E. Cheese, we couldn't find the party."

"Why couldn't you find them?" asked Maria as they stepped onto the train.

"She called the kid's mom to find out where they were,"

said Sebastian, "and his mother had no idea what my mom was talking about. Ricky's birthday wasn't until summer. It had all been a mean trick."

"That's terrible," said Maria. She felt bad for Sebastian. She'd always wanted to be around other kids—even join a team—but maybe it wasn't worth it if kids weren't nice. After a few stops, Maria said, "I think someone played a trick on me. Someone very close to me."

"Well, this is why we should stick together," said Sebastian. "Like outcasts."

Maria didn't like the sound of being an outcast, but she was beginning to warm up to Sebastian. By the time they reached Fulton, the two were able to grab seats as the train headed to Brooklyn.

When they exited the train, Maria stalled.

"Are you coming with me?" asked Sebastian.

"No," Maria said. She knew better than to let her mother see the two of them returning together. "I forgot my books at the library. You go on!" she said, motioning with her hand.

"Okay," said Sebastian. "But I think the library will be closed by the time you get there."

"I'll hurry," she said. And then she ran ahead, leaving Sebastian outside the subway station.

Maria discovered that the library was, indeed, closed, so she doubled back for home. It wasn't long before she stood outside her building. The autumn sun had sunk behind her, and a chilling wind blew leaves around. She turned the knob before the door creaked open.

She'd tell her mom she had an overdue library book. It was a flimsy excuse for being gone for so long, but since she was holding no books, it would have to do.

Maria stopped in the hallway and listened for signs of life. Distant squawks of Houdini rang between the slamming of cabinets at the far end of the apartment.

Her home felt drabber than ever. Maria dragged herself through the parlor, down the dark hallway where not a single picture hung, through her mother's bedroom where the newspaper clippings fluttered as she whooshed by. If only there were the promise of hot tea whistling in the next room.

She paused before the only thing that gave her hope: a poster of her grandmother. For a split second, she thought her grandmother's portrait winked at her. She glanced again, at the slight smile on her grandmother's face, her warm eyes motionless. She was imagining things.

She barely remembered her grandmother. Just her soft hands on her head, tucking her in at night. And stories she'd whisper to her about the crystal blue ocean along San Juan, the home she'd left before migrating to Brooklyn. After her grandmother's death, her mother assumed her psychic title and continued the family business.

Maria took a deep breath before she pushed open the door to the kitchen.

"There's my girl!" sang Madame Destine. "You're just in time to celebrate!" She threw a bag of chips at Maria. They hit her in the chest before she fumbled and dropped them.

Madame Destine danced around the kitchen, the warm light casting jubilant shadows. She flung open the doors to the cabinets. The hinges squeaked as bags of chips, Ding Dongs, and beef jerky—more food than Maria had ever seen—spilled to the floor; the kitchen had been transformed into a cornucopia of abundance.

"The ring came through, and Fox pawned it this afternoon." Madame Destine threw her arms in the air. "What do you wanna eat for dinner, Maria? Ice cream?" She opened the freezer. "Here's a tub of chocolate mint! You don't like mint? Then cookie dough! We're saved, I tell ya! SAVED!" Madame Destine grabbed Mr. Fox by his arms and waltzed around the kitchen.

"Stealing from that lady was nothing," he said. "I was taking candy from a baby!" Mr. Fox laughed and dipped Madame Destine so low her turban scraped the floor. Houdini fluttered about the kitchen in dismay.

Maria grabbed the bag of chips from the floor and carefully opened them. She thought of the baguette she'd consumed earlier. She wasn't so hungry anymore, but she ate a few chips anyway.

"How was the library?" asked Madame Destine, releasing Mr. Fox from her embrace. Houdini settled back onto her shoulder.

Maria flinched and quickly said, "Fine."

"Oh? Find anything interesting?" She seemed only half present as she popped open the fridge. The light hummed as it displayed an array of soft drinks. Madame Destine found a cherry soda and brought it to the table. Then she poured a bag of chips into the fruit bowl and offered them to Mr. Fox and Maria.

"I ordered some books from the other branches," Maria lied. "They should arrive in a few weeks." Her shoulders were tense as she waited for another question, but her mother seemed satisfied.

"John, pass me the salsa," said Madame Destine, and crammed six more chips into her mouth, the crumbs spilling into her lap.

Madame Destine poured everyone a glass of cherry soda. Then she popped up from the table and gave a toast. "This meal could not have happened without the help of my comrades. You both have been real troupers through this." She turned to Mr. Fox and tilted her head with a warm smile. "John, you sly dog. Your delivery on the phone was impeccable, and you really came through with snatching the ring from our target."

Mr. Fox blushed, tilting his cap. "Anything for you, Destine."

"And my darling Maria." Madame Destine swung her glass of fizzy soda at her with wild, excited eyes. "My clever little student. You assisted in designing a website AND a business card. You followed your cues like a real pro. I'm SO proud of you."

The three of them clinked their cups in unison and sipped their sodas. Madame Destine was in a rare good mood, and it was contagious. Maria looked at her empty bowl. The white ceramic smiled back at her. She felt slightly guilty at celebrating over conning a poor lady out of her possession, but she shook off her worries with a scoop of cookie dough ice cream and plopped it into her bowl. Then she poured the rest of her soda over it.

But ever so faintly, a muffled noise sounded in the kitchen: *ring ring*.

"Shh! What's that?" Madame Destine brought her hand to her ear and waved the others to stop moving.

Ring ring.

"I hear it, too," said Maria.

Mr. Fox dug through his pockets and pulled out his cell phone.

RING RING! The three of them jumped.

"Answer it!" commanded Madame Destine.

Mr. Fox pressed the button and brought the phone up to his face. "Brooklyn Urban Youth Initiative for Tomorrow, this is Ben speaking."

Madame Destine watched Mr. Fox with eager eyes.

"She just stepped out to eat dinner. May I ask who's calling . . . ? Yes, then please call back another time. Goodbye."

"Who was that?" asked Madame Destine. "What did they want?"

Mr. Fox crammed his mouth full of chips and mumbled, "Someone looking for ya." He chewed a little more before he said, "An Officer O'Malley, but we're celebrating. I told 'em you were out."

Madame Destine sat very still. Her pale face boiled over into a hot fury. "An OFFICER asked for ME?"

Mr. Fox stopped chewing and slapped his forehead. "Ooops!"

Maria dropped her spoon in her bowl and held on to the bottom of her chair. The party was about to end.

"How has SOMEONE connected ME to the charity line?" she said. Madame Destine narrowed her eyes at Mr. Fox. "You told them I was out? You tell them they have the wrong number!"

Mr. Fox slapped his forehead again with his palm.

She narrowed her eyes. "No one's supposed to ask for Destine on the charity line. We're not connected, remember?"

Madame Destine swung her arms across the table, knocking the ice cream, the bowl of chips, and the sodas onto the floor. She bolted from the table and backed into the cabinets like a hunted animal cornered by her predator. "They've figured it out. They're coming for me!" Her eyes were filled with paranoia.

Maria was afraid to move, and so was Mr. Fox. They

were caught in the storm, and they would have to sit through it.

Madame Destine glared at Maria. "You been talking to someone!"

Maria broke out into a sweat. "No. No one." But suddenly Ms. Madigan and Officer O'Malley flashed before her eyes. She remembered holding the bait with the phone number, but she'd put it back in her pocket. She quickly stuffed her hand in her dirty jeans pocket, pulling out her library card and nothing else. It must have fallen out with her change! Maybe she should speak up and tell her mother it could only be Ms. Madigan, concerned for her welfare.

"Then HOW did someone ask for me on the charity line?"

"CHARITY LINE! CHARITY LINE!" squawked Houdini.

Maria sank into her chair. It was better to say nothing than to tell her the truth. She wished Edward were with her now.

"One of you has been an informant," said Madame Destine. "I will find out who has leaked our secret, and I will SQUASH YOU!"

"SQUASH YOU! SQUASH YOU!" mimicked Houdini.

Madame Destine gave Houdini a kiss. "That's right," she said. Then she took a deep breath and fluffed her coat collar. Ever so gently, she said, "But seeing as I have no proof, I'll have to suspect that the widow has put two and two together." Madame Destine approached the table, grabbing it with both hands, and leaned forward. "From now on we need to watch our backs. If you see anything strange, I want you to tell me. We keep to ourselves. We talk to no one. You hear me?"

Madame Destine backed into the doorway before she smoothed down her sweaty hair under her turban. "Mama's worked up a headache," Madame Destine whimpered before she shot a glance at Maria. "Don't disturb me!" She flung open the door and stormed into her room, slamming the door behind her.

Mr. Fox hit the table with his fist. "Who you been talking to?"

Maria shook her head. "No one."

"Don't mess this up, girl. I got a good thing going with Destine. If I find out you been talking, I'll personally see to it you never open your mouth again." Mr. Fox hit his fist in his hand, making a loud smack. Then he jerked up from the table and exited the kitchen door to the courtyard.

Maria glanced out the window at Mr. Fox, who kicked at the converted shed where he kept his tools, before disappearing inside.

Her stomach ached from all the junk food, and she was thirsty from the salty chips and the ice cream. She poured herself a glass of water from the kitchen sink and glanced around at the remains of the party. The abandoned chairs were lost in a pile of chips that had been stomped into the floor. An overturned bottle wept soda. The floor was a sticky goop of melted ice cream. She realized she had no place to go but the kitchen until her mother was sound asleep. Only then would it be safe to sneak into her closet.

Maria pulled out a broom and dustpan and tried to understand the mess that she was in.

9
Mystifying Messages

Hours later, in the still of the night, Maria squatted on her mattress in the walk-in closet. Thunderous snoring from her mother's bedroom shook her doorknob. The cool tingle of Edward settled over the back of her neck. She closed her eyes at his reassuring touch.

His presence had always comforted her, ever since his first visit when she was tiny, no older than three. That day, the light in her bedroom flickered, as if gasping for its last breath. Maria sat on her mattress. She held a pen in her hand and was scribbling back and forth on a piece of paper.

Suddenly, the light died, and Maria stared into blackness.

Before she had time to cry, something otherworldly—something cool and gentle—took over her hand and held the pen in place. Maria's tiny hand made swoops and swishes across the page while she settled into a slumber.

When she awakened some hours later, she felt around her room for the door until she found it. She turned the knob, and daylight flooded her bedroom.

Three pages of strange markings lay on the floor by her bed. Maria held the pages up to her face and examined the beautiful penmanship.

They were words!

But the young Maria couldn't read, so she begged her mother to teach her. It turned out Maria was a quick learner.

That was how it all began with her and Edward. If it wasn't for him, she would never have become a reader; she never would have found the library, Ms. Madigan, or even this new friend, Sebastian.

Maria shook her head in the dark closet. She opened her eyes to glance up at her mother's furs hovering high above her like storm clouds threatening to downpour. She swallowed and eased back on her elbows. "It's my fault! I gave her away." Maria felt Edward's cool touch on her head again.

"Edward," Maria whispered, changing the subject, "I saw her today. Mrs. Fisher." Maria brought her arm behind her and felt around her bed for some paper. She placed a sheet directly in front of her. "And I liked her. But I don't think she believed me. What should I do?" Maria felt the cool chill of Edward around her and worried he would be angry.

Cautiously, she placed the pen between her knuckles,

took a deep breath, and let her hand rest on top of the paper. She felt Edward's frosty touch moving her hand at his will, but it was not a harsh touch. When her hand stopped, Maria glanced at the message:

Pay no mind to your mother.
You'll have to disobey her
If you're to help Mrs. Fisher.
I'll write another letter
About the buried treasure.
But you must bring the riddle
To the house of Mrs. Fisher . . .

Maria read Edward's writing twice. How could she keep disobeying her mother? Madame Destine was already suspecting her of revealing the family scheme. Why couldn't Edward just tell her what she needed to know?

"Edward! I could get into a lot of trouble by visiting her again," she said. But then she yawned. Maria eased back on her mattress. It was getting late.

Edward's cool grip stung her wrist and guided it back to the paper on the floor. "Okay! I'll take it to Mrs. Fisher," Maria said in the midst of another yawn.

Maria was still perplexed about disobeying her mother. She felt along the floor for the pen. Once everything was in place, she settled back into her trance. "Okay, Edward. Tell me about the treasure."

Maria was not sure how long her hand moved back and forth. When she snapped out of her sleep, a faint band of morning light showed beneath the door. Maria found the sheet of paper on the floor filled with words:

Dizzy drove rhythmic honks through
Village streets.
Jackson dripped and flung his paint
On canvas.
Neal, Jack, and Allen beat the Times Square Hustle
With poetry.
We were the underbelly, served on the blue plate special by
The Media.
With trumpet, brush, a pen, and paper, we were well
Seasoned and delicious.
Your husband dined with us and served all on
His menu.
But you kept the candles burning long after the dinners
Had ended.
Feast your eyes on this teaser, for your main course
Is treasure.

Maria read the message four times, but it was just a jumble of words. Who were these names? And what main course was coming? Maria wasn't sure if the hidden treasure was food or gold and jewels. "Why can't you just tell me where the treasure is?" Maria said. But Edward's presence was long gone. There were only the loud snores of Madame Destine from behind the door.

Maria folded the message into a square and stuffed it inside her jeans pocket. Then she fell onto her mattress and sank into a deep sleep.

She tossed and turned under her thin blanket. Suddenly, she was standing on a stage before an audience of one person hidden in shadow. She ran her hands over her sequined sleeve under the hot spotlight.

The drums rolled, and the light blinded her. She held three items: a cell phone, a diamond ring, and a piece of paper folded into a square. She began to juggle them, but she kept dropping them and having to start over.

Paper, ring, phone, paper, ring, phone— Was she getting the hang of it? There was motion in the seats below, and the dark form approached the stage.

Clap! Clap! Clap!

The figure was clapping steadily in slow motion, the sound growing louder as it neared. But the person's face was still in shadow.

Clap! Clap! Clap!

Faster and faster Maria juggled.

Clap! Clap! Clap!

At the stage, the face fell from the shadows to reveal two bulging eyes underneath a heavy turban. Madame Destine!

"OPPORTUNITY! OPPORTUNITY!" she screeched.

Maria was confused. This was not the voice of her mother. "Who are you?" she whispered, still juggling.

Madame Destine grabbed Maria's arm and squawked, "KNOCK IT OFF! KNOCK IT OFF!"

The items Maria had juggled dropped one by one to the floor. Then a chill slid down her spine. "Houdini?"

Her mother smiled and backed away into the shadows.

Ring! Ring!

The cell phone vibrated against the wooden stage floor.

Ring! Ring!

Maria crouched to pick it up. Her hand shook as she pressed the button and brought the phone to her ear. She tried to swallow, but her mouth was dry. No words could come out. She finally managed to croak, "Hello?"

"Maria?"

Maria almost dropped the phone. "Who is this?" she whispered.

"You're quite the little performer. You almost had me fooled. Check behind the paintings." The phone went dead.

Now there was no mistaking the voice. It was Madame Destine!

Maria shot up in bed.

Her face was wet, and she was cloaked in darkness. She must have had a nightmare. The familiar scent of musty coats reassured her that she was still in her closet. She felt around her mattress for the pen and some paper. She placed the pen between her knuckles and hovered over the paper.

"E-E-E-Edward, are you there?" Her voice trembled.

The air did not stir.

"I need to know if everything is going to turn out okay!" Maria knew that her recent actions had placed her in danger, and there was no returning to the way things were.

She sank into her pillow and tried to fall back to sleep, but her eyes remained open, staring into the black void of uncertainty.

10
The Sharks Are Circling

Hunched at the computer station in the library, Maria stared down at the riddle she'd received the night before, searching for leads. Who or what was Dizzy? Jack was some kind of painter, she knew. And there were three poets with only first names. She googled: "Jack painter," "poet Allen," "Dizzy Village," but nothing came up on the screen that made any sense. Maria sighed and blew her hair from her eyes. She wanted to crack the riddle before she brought the message to Mrs. Fisher. She rubbed her eyes, then opened them again and stared straight at the screen.

Still nothing.

But there was *something*. Something moving in the corner of her vision.

Two eyes shone from behind the stack of books. Someone on the other side of the bookshelf was watching her.

Maria quickly turned her head, but the figure ducked.

She shook it off and brought the paper back in front of her. *Kids are so annoying,* she thought. She had work to do. After all, Edward had ordered her to find Mrs. Fisher's treasure. If she solved the riddle, maybe the widow would invite her inside her apartment again and feed her warm bread and butter.

Ka-thud!

Four display books toppled onto Maria. A red ball cap darted behind the shelf.

Maria whipped around. She stood up from her desk but saw nothing out of the ordinary, so she sat down again and tried to focus on her task. The library would be closing soon. She typed in "blue plate special" from Edward's strange riddle. A bunch of diners and menus popped up. Why couldn't she find anything worthwhile?

"What are you doing?" whispered a voice behind her.

Maria spun abruptly. Sebastian stood before her, grinning shyly.

"I thought I'd find you here."

"Shhhh. I'm concentrating!" Maria told him, but secretly she was glad to see him. Anything was better than trying to make sense of this blue plate whatever.

"I was thinking that I'd drop by today and get your mom to tell my fortune?"

Maria's eyes grew big. "NO! I mean . . . She's busy."

But Sebastian persisted. "How do I make an appointment? Do I just knock on the door?"

"Uh. I don't think that's a good idea," Maria's voice grew louder.

Ms. Madigan waved at her from behind her desk.

"It's just . . . She doesn't like visitors," Maria added in a whisper.

"How come? I thought she was a psychic. Doesn't she earn her living from visitors?"

"She likes GROWN-UP visitors. Not kids," Maria said.

"But I would be a paying visitor. I saved up my allowance."

"I told you no!"

Sebastian was silent for a second. "How much does she charge?"

Maria threw her hands up and slid back in her chair. She knew her mother would not like a nosy neighbor in her parlor and, even worse, a kid that lived directly upstairs. Sebastian would be camped outside her door, and Maria would surely get the blame. Finally, Maria blurted out, "It's better to just meet here."

Sebastian puffed out his lip. "If you say so. But it would be much easier to just—"

Maria pretended to ignore him and read the lines to the riddle aloud to herself. "Feast your eyes on this teaser, for your main course is treasure."

"Treasure?" Sebastian whispered. He dropped down to the seat next to Maria. "Does this have something to do with what you were going on about yesterday? About a treasure?" He snatched Edward's message from the table.

Maria shot up from her chair and swiped at the riddle, but Sebastian pulled it out of reach. His brow creased, and his lips moved silently as he read. Then he gave the message back to Maria and said, "It's just a poem."

"A poem?" Maria was annoyed. It couldn't be that simple. "It's a riddle! A clue."

Sebastian nodded. "And it's a poem." He gave an amused smirk and pointed at the lines. "I think it's a metaphor," said Sebastian. "We're learning about them in school."

"A meta-what?" asked Maria.

"My dad orders the blue plate special in diners. It's food. The poem seems like it's talking about food, but it's really talking about a group of artists. Poems are sometimes riddles because you have to decode their metaphors."

Maria blew the hair out of her eyes. "But what does it mean?"

"I suspect it has something to do with artists and poets. I don't know what Dizzy means, but I'll bet it has something to do with music."

Maria shrugged. "I knew that." Then she fell into her chair by the computer.

"Where did you get this?"

Maria turned her head to the screen. "It's a secret!" She

could see Ms. Madigan out of the corner of her eye. The librarian was watching her.

"A secret?" asked Sebastian. "Since when is a poem a secret? Who's it by, and why do you want to know what it means?"

Maria exhaled loudly before she studied Sebastian. He was smart and asked so many questions. None of them were safe to answer. But he had deciphered that the poem was about artists. And maybe the artists had something to do with the art on Mrs. Fisher's wall. Could it be that the treasure was behind a painting in Mrs. Fisher's apartment? Like she'd heard in her dream? He might have just helped her solve where the treasure was. Finally, Maria blurted out, "It's true. I'm searching for treasure. I followed the woman home yesterday because it's supposed to be hidden in her apartment. It's probably behind one of her paintings."

"No way!" Sebastian said, grabbing the riddle again. He backed his chair up with a loud screech before Maria could snatch the paper back. "Where did you get this information?"

"It's none of your business!" said Maria, flinging her arms at Sebastian while he held the riddle just out of her reach.

Sebastian folded his arms. "Then I'll knock on your door!" He waited, as if letting Maria process his threat.

But Ms. Madigan was walking straight toward them.

"Don't ever knock on my door!" Maria said, and snatched the riddle out of Sebastian's hand. "I told you my mother hates kid visitors."

The tap of Ms. Madigan's heels clicked louder against the floor as the librarian approached. Maria needed to end this conversation fast.

"Okay, I'll let you come with me to Mrs. Fisher's if you promise to never, EVER, under any circumstances, knock on my door."

"Can I call you?"

"No! I mean . . . I don't have a phone."

"Then how will I know when it's time to find the treasure?"

Maria glanced quickly at the librarian before lowering her head. "You won't."

Sebastian sighed and leaned on his elbows at the computer station. "I don't understand!"

"Hello, Maria," said Ms. Madigan.

Maria gave a forced smile. "Hi, Ms. Madigan."

"Glad to see you're talking with Sebastian. I thought you two would get along." Ms. Madigan smiled. "But I'm going to have to ask you guys to keep it down a bit."

"Sorry, Ms. Madigan." Maria sighed. "Sebastian was just leaving."

"No, I wasn't."

"No one has to leave, Maria. I'm just asking that you keep your voices down," said Ms. Madigan.

Maria stared at her sneakers. She just wanted everyone to leave so she could get back to work.

"Incidentally," Ms. Madigan began in a cautious tone,

"I noticed from the business card that fell from your pocket that your mother works for a local nonprofit." Ms. Madigan pulled out the bent business card and read, "Mr. Benjamin Edward Factor?"

"No, she doesn't," Sebastian said. He looked directly at Maria as if he had been hit across the face. "She's a psych—"

Maria kicked him under the computer station.

"Ow!"

"Are you okay?" Ms. Madigan asked Sebastian.

He nodded back.

Ms. Madigan turned her attention to Maria again. "Officer O'Malley was hoping to ask your mom some questions but couldn't reach her."

Maria began to realize that the librarian was trying to help her, but all she was doing was making things worse. Maria couldn't blow her mother's cover. If the cops came, it was over. They'd take her away, and she'd be an orphan. Madame Destine wasn't all that kind, but she'd taught Maria all she knew, and she fed her.

Maria swallowed. She looked at Ms. Madigan and then at Sebastian. "She's busy," she said to both of them.

"I know that," Ms. Madigan said with a sigh. "When would be a good time to reach her?"

Maria propelled herself from her chair and backed into a bookshelf. So many questions! She needed to get out of there.

"I thought your mother was a psychic," Sebastian said. "The sign even says so outside your—"

"Be quiet!" Maria whispered. She snatched her message from the table and pushed past Ms. Madigan and Sebastian, jetting for the entrance. She flung open the first door and hit the second one, brushing past a mother with a stroller that was lodged in the doorway.

Maria ran past the iron gates of the brownstone apartments, over the uneven slabs of sidewalk, until she finally reached her home.

There was nowhere else to go; everywhere she turned, the sharks were circling.

11
Finding a Clue

It had been a week since Maria had heard from Edward. After all of Ms. Madigan's questions, Maria had decided it was time to boycott the library—at least for now. So she spent most of her days reading under the dim light bulb in the walk-in closet. If she went outside, she'd run into Sebastian, who'd hound her about finding the treasure and surely get her in trouble with her mother.

Maria shut her eyes. Images appeared in her mind of soft curtains blowing in a window and light pouring into the living room. Tribal masks hung from walls. A black cat peeked in from the hallway. A tray with a baguette. It was the widow's apartment.

If only there was a way to tell Mrs. Fisher *everything*, but she knew the widow would never believe her. She would start asking questions just like Sebastian and Ms. Madigan. But she was certain the treasure was hidden behind a painting, like in her dream. And the poem about artists seemed to back up her hunch.

Then Maria's stomach grumbled. She forced herself off her mattress and into the kitchen. Maria opened a cabinet.

Empty.

Then another.

Empty.

The food they'd scored from the pawned wedding ring had all been eaten. Mr. Fox was always snacking between meals!

Maria dragged her feet across the floorboards through the silent home. She figured Madame Destine and Mr. Fox must be out. She dug into the pocket of her dirty jeans, hoping to find a couple of coins to purchase beef jerky at the store.

Nothing. But wait. She pulled out the MetroCard Mrs. Fisher had given her.

Well, that solves it, thought Maria. Even if Mrs. Fisher didn't believe her, she would have to be Maria's meal ticket again. Maybe the widow would offer her more of that delicious bread.

After about thirty minutes underground, Maria found herself dodging students and tourists on West Fourth Street.

The loud groans of buses and congested traffic drowned out Maria's angry stomach.

She stood outside the widow's home and rang the buzzer. Ever so faintly, the melody of piano playing drifted from the second story of the town house. The music stopped.

What if Mrs. Fisher didn't want to see her? What was she going to say when she opened the door?

Light footsteps hit the stairs, and the door slowly creaked open.

Maria's mind went blank. Without realizing what she was saying, Maria mumbled, "I . . . I . . . I have another clue."

Mrs. Fisher beamed, and every line in her face floated an inch higher. "I just *knew* you'd return! Come inside." Mrs. Fisher turned and climbed the stairs.

"I've been expecting you, and this time I'm prepared!" said Mrs. Fisher.

Maria entered the widow's apartment at the top of the stairs, breathless from the climb. The familiar smell of talcum powder and old books didn't disturb her this time. It felt good to be back again.

"Go make yourself at home in the living room," said the widow. "I'll be joining you shortly."

Maria's mouth watered at the thought of eating more bread, but she didn't care what Mrs. Fisher brought her to eat. She would stay long enough for her stomach to stop hurting, then she'd think of an exit strategy.

Maria took in the strange masks that seemed to stare down at her like an audience of cartoon ghosts. Sheet music rested in clumps on the piano bench, where Mrs. Fisher must have been playing.

"I visited the market after I saw you last," the widow said, wheeling her cart into the living room. Another baguette rested on top of it, along with slices of apples, jars of jam, and a pot of tea.

Maria smiled and attacked the tray, tearing off a large chunk of bread and stuffing it into her mouth.

"After our last visit, I decided to get the old piano tuned and try my hand at it a—" Mrs. Fisher gasped and brought her hands up to her face. "Good heavens, child! If I'd known you were *this* hungry, I'd have brought you a proper meal!"

Maria realized she must look desperate. Her mouth was full, and bread crumbs speckled her lap. She brushed them off and decided to chew her food slowly so Mrs. Fisher wouldn't ask questions. Maria swallowed her bread and dug into her pocket, unfolding the riddle Edward had given her the week before. "This is the clue," Maria said, and bit into an apple slice. "It's about artists, I think. The treasure is behind one of your paintings," she managed, with her mouth full.

"I dust these paintings every so often. I think I would know if there was something hidden behind one." Mrs. Fisher's eyes traveled over the message several times.

Maria swallowed the apple. *Now what?* she thought, and poured some tea. Mrs. Fisher put on a record where a wild trumpet spun behind her voice on the scratchy disk.

The black cat hopped from the table of books and meandered his way to the cart with food. Maria placed the cup on the trunk and waited for Mrs. Fisher to look up from Edward's clue.

Finally, Mrs. Fisher brought the paper down before adjusting her glasses.

"Well, is it a clue?" asked Maria. "Something to do with the stuff on your walls?"

"Where . . . did you get this?" asked Mrs. Fisher.

"I told you—a friend."

"Yes, I know. How *old* is your friend? He's not a boy, is he?"

Maria tensed. "I'm not sure, exactly. Why?"

"Come now, Maria, you show up out of nowhere and then you bring me *this*."

Maria popped off the sofa and began to study a mask that hung on the other side of the living room. The face was round and funny, with two tiny dots for eyes and a giant mouth. Maria wasn't sure what to say. Telling Mrs. Fisher about Edward seemed risky.

"How did this message come into your hands?" said Mrs. Fisher.

"My friend gave it to me."

"What does this *friend* look like?"

Maria tilted her head at a skinny mask with floppy whiskers. "I don't know. I've never seen his face. We talk, but I . . . I don't know much more about him.

"This handwriting looks unusual. It's old-fashioned. Is he a teacher? A neighbor? A relative?"

"I don't have any relatives," Maria said without any emotion. "Well, except for my mom and Mr. Fox."

Mrs. Fisher's cat rubbed against Maria's leg. Maria swooped down to pick him up and caught her reflection in the large full-length mirror not far from the piano. Maria imagined that the cat was hers.

"What's your cat's name?" she asked.

"Archimedes," replied Mrs. Fisher in the mirror's reflection. "This poem seems familiar to me, and I may very well know the man that sent it."

"I don't think that you do. Edward would have told me," said Maria. She let go of the cat, wiping off the fur from her shirt.

"Edward?" Mrs. Fisher said quickly.

Maria froze. She hadn't meant to mention Edward. A wailing trumpet cut through the silence while she tried to think of an answer. Maria needed to keep her mouth shut. *Just focus on the treasure*, she told herself.

Mrs. Fisher poured Maria more tea. "And what is his last name?" she asked.

Maria took the tea and retreated back to the wall with masks. Mrs. Fisher eased off the sofa and flattened her skirt.

"I've known a lot of artists and writers in my life," she told Maria, and moved closer to her.

"I don't know his last name," Maria said. She darted to the open window by the sofa and peered over the street. A couple of people were talking below. A cab honked, and a bus screeched to a halt. Then Maria groaned. Standing at the corner below, in his red ball cap, was Sebastian.

Maybe it was a bad idea that she came.

"I don't mean to frighten you, Maria. No more questions, then," said Mrs. Fisher. "Let's enjoy our tea." She clapped her hands and motioned Maria back to the sofa. Then she offered her some more slices of apples on a tray.

The two eased back onto the sofa. Mrs. Fisher pointed to the record player. "You hear that trumpet?" she asked.

Maria shrugged. "Sure."

"That's Dizzy. Dizzy Gillespie. He was a jazz musician, and he's the first mentioned in the poem."

Maria nodded. "Did he play in the Village?"

"Yes," said Mrs. Fisher. "The Village Vanguard, and it's not far from here. Perhaps you should look for your treasure there."

※　※　※

Maria stepped outside Mrs. Fisher's building into the sunny autumn morning.

Sebastian jerked his head up from his phone at the slam

of the door. "You were supposed to take me along with you! I'm the one helping you, remember?"

Maria sighed. "Sorry. I got another clue at Mrs. Fisher's, but I actually do need your help this time."

Sebastian shoved his phone into his pocket, then slowly leaned against the facade of Mrs. Fisher's building. "So NOW you need me," he said, folding his arms.

Maria exhaled. Then she looked away for a second. "Okay. What do you want?"

"I want half."

"Half of what?" Maria laughed.

"The treasure. If I help you, then we're partners."

"Partners? Ha! It's not MY treasure. It's Mrs. Fisher's. I'm only helping her—"

"Partners," Sebastian said louder, with a nod. "There's no 'Oh, sorry I forgot to take you with me to find the treasure, Sebastian' or 'Go away. My mom hates visitors, Sebastian.'"

"She does hate visitors!"

"I don't care!" Sebastian stood upright.

Maria was surprised at how tough Sebastian could appear when he was angry.

"Look. If we're gonna be a team, you have to keep me in the loop. I'm not gonna get stuck with a raw deal."

"Fine," Maria said. "We're partners, then."

"Pinkie swear," Sebastian said, holding out his smallest finger for Maria to shake.

"What's this?"

"Hold out your pinkie."

Maria extended a pale fifth digit and locked it into Sebastian's.

"Okay," Sebastian said. "We're good."

"Then get your phone and pull up directions to the Village Vanguard."

12
Culture Vultures

Sebastian and Maria hiked up Sixth Avenue, passing the West Fourth Street subway stop. A crowd cheered when a basketball made it through the net in the fenced-in court. Maria paused at the corner to consider a street vendor's books again, but Sebastian pulled her away. They turned left, walking up West Fourth Street, until it hit Seventh Avenue. Sebastian checked the GPS, and they turned right. After stopping to pet a Pomeranian on his walk, Sebastian and Maria arrived under the red awning of the Village Vanguard.

"Now what?" Sebastian asked. "The place doesn't look like it's open."

Maria beat on the door.

Nothing.

They waited for a few minutes before the door creaked

open and a young woman with short red hair pulled out a heavy sack of trash.

"Excuse me," said Maria. "We're on a mission to find a treasure, and one of the clues is to search the Vanguard."

The young woman ignored Maria while she hefted the sack and wobbled to the curb before dropping it on the street. "SHEEESH!" She exhaled and wiped the sweat from her brow. After a moment, she acknowledged them, and said, "Oh . . . are you kids on a scavenger hunt?"

Sebastian shrugged. "Sure."

"I didn't know we were back on the list. And usually it's college kids competing with one another," she said. "But that's cool." She jiggled her keys before opening the front door. "We don't open until the evening, but the owner's out. I'll give you five minutes to find the clue."

Maria couldn't believe her luck. They followed behind the woman into the dark club, where they descended a bunch of stairs and entered a cramped basement. The woman disappeared before the overhead lights flickered on one at a time.

The space was triangular, with the narrowest part a raised stage containing a piano and a few microphones. Red curtains draped against the wall of the stage. The rest of the club was packed tightly with tables and chairs. The walls were filled with black-and-white photos of musicians, and an old horn rested in between the photos. Maria could detect a musty smell mixed with the scent of pine soap in the mop bucket.

"What are we looking for down here?" whispered Sebastian.

"Either Dizzy Gillespie or some kind of clue," said Maria. "Let's start with the photos." Men with saxophones and women in ruffled tops and tight skirts danced in some of the images lining the wall. Maria pushed some chairs aside to get a closer look.

"Where's the bathroom?" Sebastian asked.

"How should I know?" said Maria. "Did you ask the lady who let us in?"

Sebastian jetted past the tables to the back, turning a corner and knocking a photo off the wall.

SMASH!

Maria and Sebastian stopped.

Then Maria darted across the room to the fallen photo. "Go, clumsy!" Maria said, shooing Sebastian with her hand. "I'll clean it up before she finds out." Maria squatted and carefully lifted the frame from the floor. Shards of glass hit the ground, and the photo slipped away from the frame.

Maria turned the picture over to discover a group of men in suits seated at a table. There was a woman seated next to an older, balding man. The two figures looked familiar to Maria, like the couple in the photo in Mrs. Fisher's apartment. Maria turned the photo over to discover some cursive writing in blue ink.

To Max,
May your doors stay open from here to eternity.
From your pals,
Neal, Jack, Allen, and the Fishers

It was Mrs. Fisher! Maybe this was the clue they were looking for! Maria dug Edward's riddle out of her pocket and read it again:

Neal, Jack, and Allen beat the Times Square Hustle
With poetry.

Squish. Squish. Squish.

Squeaky sneakers on a sticky floor crept up behind Maria. She turned around.

"What did you find?" asked Sebastian, now calm after his bathroom run.

"Look," said Maria. "The names of these men at the table are the same ones in the poem."

"Do you think this is what the poem was talking about?" asked Sebastian.

"It could be," said Maria. "The lady at the table is Mrs. Fisher."

They heard a dustpan hit the floor. "All right, kids," said the young woman who'd let them in. "Time's up. I gotta send you back—" She stopped and then her voice sank. "Uh-oh! What happened?"

"There was a small accident," said Maria. "But do you know who these people are?"

The young woman sighed and snatched the photo from Maria. After a few seconds, she said, "Sure do," and handed it back. "They're Beat poets. Studied them in school. That's Jack Kerouac," she said, tapping the face of a dark, handsome man seated in the middle. "And the guy with the glasses is most likely Allen Ginsberg."

"I knew it!" said Maria. "BEAT the Times Square Hustle! Another clue from the riddle. We're so close to finding the treasure."

The young woman ran her hand through her hair. "Four years of school and a degree in comparative literature, and now I'm helping kids on a scavenger hunt. What a riot!" She turned around and retrieved a broom. "By the way. This is a jazz venue, not a bookstore," she said, and started sweeping. "If you're looking for poets, I suggest you go to the library and let me clean up this mess."

"I'm sorry about the frame," said Maria. "Would it be okay if we took a picture of the photo?"

The woman shrugged. "Sure, I guess." She swept the glass into the dustpan and emptied it into the can.

Sebastian positioned his phone over the photo until it was in focus and took a snapshot.

"Okay, out you go," said the woman, and ushered the kids up the stairs. She opened the door before pausing. "I . . . actually, wrote a paper on Kerouac while in school. There's a bunch of stuff on him and the other poets in the Berg Collection at the New York Public Library on Forty-Second Street. That's where I'd start if you're looking for the Beat poets." Then she closed the door behind them.

"Now what?" asked Sebastian as they took a few steps away from the building. It was lunchtime, and Maria was distracted by the smell of pizza from Two Boots.

"Well, there wasn't much of anything at the club except for the poets. My guess is we should follow the lady's advice and find out more about them."

"Okay," said Sebastian. "Let me look up directions to the New York Public Library," He typed something into his phone before he pushed up his glasses. "Let's take the F train at Sixth Avenue to Bryant Park."

After a quick train ride, Sebastian and Maria climbed the stairs to find themselves in front of Bryant Park. A cool breeze caused Maria to zip up her hoodie. The park was full of tourists having a bite to eat or hunched over their phones at the tables under the trees.

They hiked the sidewalk along Forty-Second Street, stepping on brown leaves and spilt food from the vendors lining the block. First, they found the side of the giant library. Then they trudged the rest of the block until they reached the front of the building on Fifth Avenue. Maria gasped at the two stone lions guarding the stairs leading to the entrance.

"Race you up!" she said.

They took off up the stairs, Sebastian falling behind her. Maria reached the top first and slipped through the heavy doors. A panting Sebastian trailed, having trouble getting through the door. "No fair," he said. "You didn't give me a warning!"

After inquiring about the Berg collection, they were directed to room 320. They approached the desk and waited for a librarian to notice them.

"May I help you?" asked a man in his mid-thirties, with hair perfectly parted, and sporting a pink bow tie.

"We're researching Beat poets for school and wanted to check out what you have," Sebastian said. "Isn't there a special collection?"

"Well, you're in luck," replied the librarian. "This is THE center for Beat research, but I'm afraid you're going to have to make an appointment." His eyes darted up and down Maria and Sebastian as if he was trying to size them up.

"We're looking for information about Jack Kerouac," said Maria as confidently as she could.

"Well, there are books that he's written that you can check out from the regular library,"

"We're looking for a private collection, something that will give us a better clue," said Sebastian. "Personal photos, even."

"Well—er, the collection is not exactly for kids," said the librarian. "We would have to retrieve it and bring it up to you." He straightened his tie before adding, "And it's really more for scholars. Now, if you'll excuse me, we try to only see scholars who make appointments."

Maria grew uneasy. This couldn't be a dead end. "Show him the photo on your phone," she said, nudging Sebastian.

He pulled out his phone and brought it up to the librarian. "We found a picture of Jack Kerouac and Allen Ginsberg at the Village Vanguard," said Sebastian.

"And seated with Mrs. Fisher, who I personally know," added Maria.

"A photo of him at the Vanguard!" said the librarian, his face lighting up. He took the phone and examined the photo.

"Yes," said Sebastian. "And we're trying to locate something valuable for Mrs. Fisher, and this may be our only clue."

The librarian paused for a second to think. Then he said, "Wait here a minute."

After ten minutes, he appeared holding a box. "Follow

me, kids. I'll give you a quick show-and-tell, but DON'T TOUCH ANYTHING."

They trailed behind the librarian until they stood at a table with a lamp at the far end of the research room. The librarian put on cloth gloves and carefully removed the lid to the box. He reached in and pulled out old black-and-white photos and papers covered with type and scrawled handwriting. He held them as if they were made of delicate glass, capable of breaking at the slightest movement. "Now, you say he was friends with a Mrs. Fisher?"

Maria nodded.

"We don't really have her in here—that I know of. You know, Jack was married three times." The librarian continued to pull out more stuff from the box: some old drawings that looked like book cover sketches, a scroll filled with tons of text, more photos, and stacks of manuscripts with Xs drawn through them.

"What's with the scroll?" asked Sebastian.

The librarian stopped. As if he was holding his most prized jewel, he carefully unrolled the scroll, revealing a continual flow of words. "Kerouac wrote in a stream of consciousness," said the librarian, excitement bubbling in his voice. "He'd adopted Eastern spirituality and believed he could channel a manuscript's truest form through one take, without stopping for any revision."

"So he typed all that out, without knowing what he

was going to say and without messing up?" Sebastian asked, clearly impressed.

"Well," said the librarian, a slight smile forming, "it was more like he kept going. The same thing was happening with jazz improvisation at the time," he said, before rolling the script and placing it in the box. "Rumor has it that there's more work by Kerouac and other Beat poets, like Allen Ginsberg, missing from our collection. We've been unable to locate the materials." The librarian held the phone with the photo of the Fishers with the poets. "You said you visited the Village Vanguard, right? Well, it makes sense that Kerouac and Ginsberg were there, considering their philosophy was close to the way the musicians would keep playing. Sometimes it came together, other times it didn't. But when it did, you really had something."

"But what does Kerouac or Ginsberg have to do with the Fishers?" asked Maria.

"That I don't know," said the librarian.

"Do you know who Jackson is with his paint in this riddle?" asked Maria.

The librarian flattened the note and carefully read it. "It could be talking about Jackson Pollock," he said. He tapped the note a few times. "He was considered an abstract expressionist and was from that time period."

"Where can we see his paintings?" asked Sebastian.

The librarian paused to consider. "Probably the Museum of Modern Art. If you take a left out of the library and walk about ten blocks north, then take a left onto Fifty-Third, you'll find it."

Sebastian pulled Maria aside. "Do you think we should go?"

Maria shrugged. "I mean, have we found what we're looking for here? There doesn't seem to be any treasure or anything having to do with Mrs. Fisher in the collection."

"Beats me," said Sebastian. "Get it? As in BEAT POET."

Maria groaned. The Vanguard had left them with one clue: Mrs. Fisher was friends with the poets. But there was nothing at the library about Mrs. Fisher or her treasure. It appeared that the next place to look would have to be the museum. And maybe there would be a clue in one of Jackson Pollock's paintings. "Yeah," Maria said. "Let's go."

* * *

The Museum of Modern Art was jam-packed with visitors. A group of older people crowded the ticket counter while a baby cried by the bathroom. College kids sat around a bench with drawing pads. People speaking in all different languages passed Maria and Sebastian as they stood in line for their tickets.

"Looks like we're in luck," said Sebastian, reading the sign. "Children under sixteen get in free."

After they got their passes and showed them to the guard, Sebastian and Maria climbed the first flight of stairs.

They found a volunteer at the information desk by the escalators. "Can you tell us how to find a painting by Jackson Pollock?" asked Maria.

"Of course," said the woman wearing a geometric sweater. She pulled out a map and drew an X. "Go up to the permanent collection on the fourth floor."

The kids ascended the escalators and weaved through the galleries, passing an encaustic painting by Jasper Johns, a large pop art painting by Andy Warhol, and a giant comic panel by Roy Lichtenstein. After they asked a guard to point them in the direction of the Pollock painting, they found it—*One: Number 31, 1950.*

The two of them stood motionless before the painting.

Sebastian said nothing, He pursed his lips as if in deep concentration, taking in the rhythmic splatter of paint applied to the seventeen-foot canvas.

"It's a complete mess!" said Maria.

"It looks like organisms under a microscope," said Sebastian. "And look how big it is."

"I don't believe it. This was our last hope!" said Maria. She pulled out the riddle and studied it for a second before looking up. "I was hoping it contained an image I would recognize from the poem. A clue. A map. SOMETHING that would lead to the treasure." She sat down on a bench, exhausted. "I have to go back to Mrs. Fisher and tell her we're at a dead end."

"Okay, I'm coming with you," Sebastian said. But then

he checked his phone. "Shoot. My mom texted an hour ago. I gotta go home. She's wondering where I am."

Maria paused to consider how much trouble she was probably in, but she didn't have a phone for anyone to tell her. What would another hour do to her if she visited Mrs. Fisher?

They sprinted out of the museum and hurried onto the train. On the ride to Mrs. Fisher's, something didn't sit right with Maria. What was it that these artists all had in common? And why would Edward send her a riddle about artists, but have none of them lead her to treasure?

13
Automatic Writing

Maria was breathless from climbing the stairs when she entered Mrs. Fisher's apartment. She charged down the hallway to the living room and waited for Mrs. Fisher to return from the kitchen.

"How was your day?" asked the voice of the widow, who was setting something heavy on a tray in the kitchen.

"Looooong," said Maria. Archimedes poked his head out from under the couch. Then Mrs. Fisher breezed into the living room with a tray and tea.

"Did you find any clues at the Vanguard?" she asked while she poured Maria a fresh cup.

Maria fell onto the sofa and sighed. "No." She stretched her arms over the cushions. "We saw the Beats at the library—Jack Kerouac. And then we trekked up to the museum to see a painting by Jackson Pollock, but it was just splattered paint." She pulled herself upright and grabbed the tea, deciding to cradle it in her lap. "I saw a younger version of you with the Beats in a photo at the Vanguard," she said. "But I don't see what it has to do with buried treasure in your apartment."

Mrs. Fisher took a sip of tea. "Robert and I were friends with them. They were *Beat poets,* to be precise," Mrs. Fisher added. "Although they hated being labeled beatniks once it became popular."

Maria nodded. "I know they were Beat poets. I read about it in the library: Jack's giant scrolls of writing."

Archimedes jumped on the sofa with Maria, and she brushed her fingers through his fur. Then the cat pawed her and hopped off.

"After we were married, my husband ran a small press called the Hungry Ghost, publishing artists and poets with limited printings."

"Like it says in the poem?" Maria uncrumpled Edward's message and read, "Your husband dined with us and served all on his menu."

Archimedes strutted up to the dining room table and jumped onto a chair before settling onto the books lying on the table.

"Correct," said Mrs. Fisher. "They all sat at this table you see before you. Even then it was covered in books. We lived here in the Village back when the neighborhood was thriving with all kinds of artists. I'd step out for an espresso and bump into the writers William Burroughs, Carl Solomon,

Neal Cassady, or Frank O'Hara." The widow paused and smiled. "There were musicians like Charlie Parker, and the artists like Larry Rivers or illustrators like William Steig. And I'd wear my black turtlenecks and leotards. We stayed up all night discussing art, poetry, politics—everything. My husband taught at the university nearby. Over the years, he'd surround himself with his students and continue the tradition long after the Beat movement ended."

"Wait," said Maria. "Come with me!" She led Mrs. Fisher down the hall to the entrance and pointed at a picture of Mrs. Fisher surrounded by people in a cafe. "Are these your friends? The poets."

"Yes," said Mrs. Fisher. "The poem is written by a poet, but not one of the Beats mentioned. I don't know who. We had student poets over well into the late 1990s, just before my husband's death. That's why I asked you his last name. He MUST be someone I knew from over the years."

"What about the painter, then?" asked Maria, "Did you know him, too? The splatter paint guy?"

"Jackson Pollock? Not personally," said Mrs. Fisher, guiding Maria back to the living room. "But, you see—" She placed her tea on the trunk and reached for an art book on the table. "You have to train your eye." She opened the book and sat down next to Maria on the sofa. Then she thumbed through it until she found a painting. "Remember that wild melody you heard me playing by Dizzy this morning?"

Maria vaguely remembered the whirring of a trumpet

on the scratchy record. "Yeah, it was wild. I get why they called him Dizzy."

"And look at the way the paint is applied to Pollock's canvas."

Maria stared at the rhythmic swoops of paint. It flowed and splattered. It dripped and meandered. It DID kind of resemble jazz. "Okay, I think I get it," she said. "But if all of these artists were related somehow, what do they have to do with buried treasure?"

"That I don't know. Maybe your friend was some kind of artist and knew them?" Mrs. Fisher stood up and clapped her hands. "Archimedes! Down!"

The cat replied with a grumpy meow. Then he hopped off the table.

Maria shook her head. "But I don't know who Edward was before he di—" Maria stopped and looked at her shoes.

"Was?" Mrs. Fisher asked quickly. "Before he . . . what?"

Archimedes's tail knocked over an empty cup from the trunk.

"Dear Lord, you're talking to a . . . *ghost*, aren't you?" Mrs. Fisher grabbed the cup and placed it upright. Then she brushed the cat aside.

Maria looked away.

Mrs. Fisher walked around the sofa and shut the window. Then she returned to her seat next to Maria, rubbing her arms as if she was cold. "I've been trying to contact

Robert through psychics and mediums for many years," she said. "Sometimes they seem to channel him, but it's always vague. I've relied on faith that he was watching over me. But none of these mediums ever supplied me with as much proof of him as you."

Maria wasn't sure whether she should confirm or stay silent. She decided to say nothing.

"Behind a mask. You said this morning. You never see him, yet he knows so much about my past. How are you talking to him?" Mrs. Fisher placed her hand on Maria's shoulder. "Please show me."

"I don't know what—"

"Please, Maria," said Mrs. Fisher. Her voice was soft and low, full of yearning. "Tell me how you've come across my dear Robert."

Maria lifted her head. She knew what yearning felt like—the need to connect with someone. She often felt that way about Edward. And there was a time she'd felt that way for her mother, long ago. Perhaps it was okay to tell just *one* person her secret. Maria sighed. She wasn't getting anywhere helping the widow find her treasure by being vague. Maria leveled her gaze, meeting Mrs. Fisher's blue eyes. "Promise you won't tell a soul?"

"You have my word."

"May I have a fresh sheet of paper and a pen?"

"Certainly." Mrs. Fisher opened a cupboard and pulled

out a thin sheet of notebook paper. Then she fumbled around on the table until she found a pen that worked. "Will this do?"

Maria nodded and slid the books across the dining room table to make a space for her paper. Then she placed the pen between her knuckles and waited. "Edward?" she said. To her relief, the air grew cool around her. "Mrs. Fisher wants to speak with you. Can you tell her something she needs to hear?"

Mrs. Fisher cleared her throat, placing her hand on the back of Maria's chair.

Maria felt the cool touch of Edward's hand. She shut her eyes, tilted her head back, and let her pen do the magic.

Maria opened her eyes again. The pen lay flat on the table, and the warmth had returned to her hand, but the paper was gone. She turned around.

Mrs. Fisher was clutching the message, her eyes watery and her mouth moving. "I don't believe it," she said. "Automatic writing."

"Auto-what?" Maria asked, shaking her head to clear it.

"Your method is called *automatic writing*. The spiritualists used it in the nineteenth century." The paper trembled in Mrs. Fisher's hand. "They channeled ghosts through the method that you just showed me."

"Okay, but what did Edward tell you?"

Mrs. Fisher ignored her and studied the paper once again, adjusting her glasses. "The Surrealists later practiced it to tap into their unconscious. And yes, Kerouac wrote from a stream of consciousness on his scroll. And back in my jazz days, some musicians believed they were channeling the divine through improvisations, which is a musical stream of consciousness."

Maria pondered the possibility that maybe these artists were all talking to their own Edwards. It was possible. But what did they have to do with gold and jewels? Maria reached for the piece of paper. "What does it say?"

Mrs. Fisher pulled it away and smiled. "It contains specific directions to me. I must go to the kitchen and see about your snack."

"What?" Maria asked. Edward had never talked about snacks with her before.

"See for yourself." Mrs. Fisher handed the paper to Maria and then drifted down the hall.

"Meow!" Archimedes tilted his head at Maria.

She snatched the paper from the table and rubbed her free hand along the cat's back. She was beginning to like Archimedes.

Then Maria read the message:

Maria is passionate
for midday snacks.

Search the cabinets
For gingersnaps.

Maria felt her cheeks burn. Edward was making fun of her! And what were gingersnaps anyway?

Some glass and heavy objects slapped hard surfaces in the other room.

Maria dashed down the long hallway. When she found the kitchen, Mrs. Fisher was kneeling on the floor, surrounded by boxes and jars of food. Finally, the widow pulled a box of gingersnaps covered in cobwebs and dust from the back of the pantry.

"Good Lord!" Mrs. Fisher exclaimed, laughing. "Oh, Maria, I hope you didn't want *these* gingersnaps!"

"Why?" Maria asked peering at the box.

"By the look of it, they've been buried in my pantry for over thirty years! They're no good!"

Maria scrunched up her face.

Mrs. Fisher playfully shook the box at Maria's feet. "Hungry?"

Archimedes pawed at the box and cocked his head.

"Go on! Eat it! I dare you," said Maria.

Archimedes sniffed the box, then darted from the kitchen and down the hall.

Mrs. Fisher laughed and rose stiffly from the floor. She steadied herself on the kitchen island and dropped the box of cookies into the trash can. "You know, I'm a terrible homemaker. But before you return, I promise to have done some spring cleaning!"

Maria smiled and bent to replace boxes of spaghetti, cans of tomatoes, and packages of black-eyed peas back in the pantry.

"I don't know if there is buried treasure in my home," said Mrs. Fisher. "Perhaps the treasure is this talent you have for writing. You seem to share it with all the other artists on the list."

Archimedes poked his head back in the kitchen as if to see if it was safe to return.

Maria thought for a moment about whether she did possess a rare talent that was worth something. Automatic writing couldn't be very lucrative, could it? But she remembered something the librarian had said about the missing books by Jack Kerouac and other poets. Could those books be worth something? "Hey. Where would you go to find old, rare, or missing books in this town?" asked Maria.

"I don't know," said Mrs. Fisher. She strummed her fingers on the counter. "Maybe the rare book room at the Strand?"

"The Strand?" asked Maria.

"It's the largest used bookstore in the city," Mrs. Fisher said.

The afternoon sunlight moved gently over the copper

teakettle and the checkered linoleum floor. Maria knew she would *definitely* come back after she checked out the Strand.

Mrs. Fisher gently stroked the cat and smiled.

Maria decided right then and there that Mrs. Fisher could be trusted.

She might even be her *friend*.

14
Mutiny

aria jumped up the stairs and departed the subway station. The sky had faded from a fair day to a purple bruise. One by one, lights flicked on inside the apartments and mansion windows lining Clinton Avenue. Maria turned a corner and ran up her block, but then she stopped in front of her brownstone.

The upstairs windows beamed a warm yellow. Lively shadows of heads moved inside the glow. She wondered if any of them belonged to Sebastian.

Sighing, she turned the cold knob of her front door, but it resisted. The parlor windows stared back at her, dark and solemn. The heavy curtains inside were purple and swollen, blocking out any sign of life inside.

Maria rang the doorbell and waited. An autumn chill crept inside her hoodie. She shivered and pulled the zipper up to her chin. Footsteps pounded inside, growing louder until they stopped at the entrance.

The door slowly cracked open, and two eyes stared down on Maria.

"Where were you? The library is closed," said Madame Destine, her pale face resembling one of Mrs. Fisher's masks in the moonlight.

"I *was* at the library, but—"

"Get inside!" Madame Destine grabbed Maria by the arm and pulled her into the apartment. She released Maria and deadbolted the door. Then she parted the heavy curtains and jerked her head left and right. "Who you been talking to?"

Maria rubbed her arm. "No one, I told you."

Madame Destine slowly turned around to face Maria and narrowed her eyes. "You weren't at the library, I checked." Her red lips formed an eerie smile. "Now, tell me the truth!"

Maria tried to calm her shaky fingers. She unzipped her hoodie and forced herself to breathe naturally. Quickly, she came up with an excuse. "I was there . . . but after a while, I went for a walk around Fort Greene Park. I sat on the steps of the monument and read until it got too cold, then I returned the book in the drop box because the library was closed."

Maria smiled to herself. She was proud of her lie. It was unlikely that Madame Destine walked all the way to the park to look for her.

"Who did you talk to in the park?" Madame Destine pried, folding her arms over her chest.

"No one."

"No one . . . was following you?"

"Not that I know of." Maria said with a shrug. She knew she needed to get away from her mom's questions, so she backed into the master bedroom and opened the door to her closet.

But Madame Destine blocked the entrance. "Oh, we're not done!" she said, and grabbed Maria by the wrist, pushing her in the opposite direction. "Go to the kitchen!"

Maria stumbled into the kitchen and blinked in the bright light.

Mr. Fox swung his head around from the cupboards. "Oh, there she is," he said. He appeared to be packing boxes with dishes. "Out double-crossing your own kind?"

"I don't know what you—"

"Silence!" said Madame Destine.

Houdini flapped his wings on Madame Destine's shoulder.

"John has been getting more phone calls," said Madame Destine. "Now it's a woman's voice. They're looking for me. Probably have the phone tapped."

"Who?" Maria asked. She found it hard to believe that Ms. Madigan had tapped her house.

"Don't play coy with me, Maria. The police!"

Maria knew she should tell her mother about Officer

O'Malley questioning her and the bait falling out of her pocket, but she didn't want to send her mom into a rage. "Are you *sure* they're onto your scam? Did they tell you what they want? Maybe it's about something else. Just talk to them," said Maria.

"Don't be foolish. Of course they're onto the scam!" said Madame Destine. "How else could they deduce that I'm connected with the number?"

"You stupid kid," said Mr. Fox. "You think you know everything!" He bit off a chunk of duct tape and wrapped it around a box.

Maria knew it was definitely too late to tell her mother about the library newsletter photo. Besides. She'd never believe that the librarian was really after her signature. But Ms. Madigan was *hardly* a threat. Surely it would all blow over! "I think you're overreacting," said Maria.

"Overreacting? A police officer asked to speak to me. We're gonna have to always be watching our backs now." Madame Destine sighed, falling into her chair at the table. "Besides, this city has gotten far too expensive to piece together a living from small cons. Now's as good a time as any to relocate. It's time to move."

"We're moving?" Maria asked. She took in the boxes in the kitchen and Mr. Fox packing. "But why? Where will we go?" Maria tried to imagine living someplace else. Would she be able to see Mrs. Fisher? And what about Sebastian and her library?

"Well, we have two options if we stay: starve on small cons or do jail time. Do you want me to go to jail?" asked Madame Destine.

"Aye!" agreed Mr. Fox. "Your own dear mother." His lips curled.

Madame Destine crept delicately behind Maria, placing her hands on her shoulders. "What will happen to you if we're caught, Maria?"

Maria shrugged, but the warmth of her mother's hands caressed her shoulders, reminding her of the times she had been sick or unhappy and Destine had taken care of her.

"*You* are a minor, so *you* are off the hook," said Madame Destine. "But Fox and I will do time."

"DO TIME! TIME!" echoed Houdini.

Madame Destine stopped rubbing Maria's shoulders and placed her hands on the back of her chair. Houdini beat his wings. "Who will take care of *you* if we're sent away?" Madame Destine asked in a sweet tone. "Who will be there to cheer you up with an ice cream sundae when things are looking gloomy?" Madame Destine crept around the chair so that their eyes met. "Who will be there to pat you on the back for a job well done when you follow your cues and the con is a success?"

Maria tried to imagine a different life. One without a parent. The thought terrified her. She'd been told about her unstable father, who'd left them penniless before he disappeared when she was a baby. Maria couldn't lose her mother, too. Her eyes began to well up, but she lifted her chin proudly so she could show her mother that she hadn't broken her spirit.

"Do you want to be put in foster care?" Madame Destine asked softly, tilting her turban toward Maria. "This life may not be all daisies and buttercups, but you know what? I've been true to you in good times and bad."

Maria trembled. "I don't want foster care." She wiped her eyes and sniffed. "Nothing's gonna happen to us! I swear!"

Madame Destine stared at her daughter intently. "Grow up!" she said, and brushed Maria off with her hand. "I don't know who you been talking to, or where you've been disappearing, but it's gonna stop!"

Maria didn't want to leave her library and her familiar sidewalk. She'd miss the tiny closet she'd known for as long as she could remember. And then there were Sebastian upstairs and Mrs. Fisher. She'd miss the widow's kindness.

"It's too late to change what's been done," Madame Destine said. "We've got to move, and it's all your fault.

"YOUR FAULT! YOUR FAULT!" mimicked Houdini.

Maria backed into some boxes.

Madame Destine smoothed down her dress before she reached for a box. "Don't think this is all there is," she said.

Maria took a deep breath and rushed for her closet.

"Double-crossing little . . ." muttered Mr. Fox.

Maria slammed her door and flung herself onto her

dingy mattress. "Edward?" she whispered, her voice trembling. "Please, are you there, Edward?" But the air remained still and stale.

Maria lay in the dark closet and stared at the blob of hanging coats. She realized there was no going back to the way things were. She was in this mess far too deep.

15
Making Contact

The next day, Maria headed to the library. She was going to miss this place when she moved. She scanned the front desk for Ms. Madigan, but she must have been at lunch, which gave Maria time to do her research.

She spread the *New York Times*, open to the obituaries, and carefully wrote down the names of every person listed. Then she made diagrams of family trees with corresponding fortunes. She needed to have an understanding of who possessed what, and where a fortune might go once a relative had *kicked the bucket*. Maybe if Maria discovered another con to buy them time, her mom would be less inclined to move. After all, they were in no real danger of being discovered by the authorities.

Maria thought this work quite dull. She drew a face of an elderly woman in the margins of her notebook and gave her glasses like Mrs. Fisher's and even that plaid cape she'd worn the day Maria followed her home. Maria wondered when she would see her friend again.

She whispered the word *friend*. It sounded lovely.

She leaned back in her chair. She still needed to visit the Strand to see if there were lost books by the Beat poets. If only Edward would send her another clue! But even if she had an excuse to see Mrs. Fisher, she'd still have to sneak out. Her mother would never let her go.

Maria sensed that she was being watched again. She snapped out of her thoughts and quickly turned in her chair. There, observing her every move, was Sebastian. He was nosier than Ms. Madigan!

"Hey, Sebastian," Maria said. "You spying?"

"I wasn't spying on you. I was WATCHING you," Sebastian said, coming out from behind the bookshelf. "I was trying to figure out why you were reading about dead people in the paper."

Maria could tell that he was holding something behind his back. She stretched her neck to peer around him, but Sebastian moved with her. "What do you have there?" she asked him.

"I—well, you said not to contact you by phone or by knocking on your door, right?"

Maria nodded.

"Well, you didn't actually say not to contact you AT ALL, so I brought you one of these." Sebastian pulled his hands from behind his back and held out a purple-and-green plastic device with a dinosaur on it.

It was a toy, and it was clearly for *little* kids. Maria rolled her eyes. "Why this?"

"It's a walkie-talkie," said Sebastian. He puffed out his chest and flashed his gap-toothed smile.

Maria reluctantly took the light piece of plastic from Sebastian. It resembled a cell phone but had no numbers on it. "How does it work?" she asked.

"You've never *seen* one of these?" Sebastian asked, tilting his head as if he didn't believe her.

Maria narrowed her eyes. "I'm homeschooled, okay?"

"Okay, okay. I get it now." Sebastian held up the device. "You switch on the knob to turn up the volume and press the button to speak. Try it."

Maria pressed the button and said, "Like this?" She heard her voice come out of Sebastian's walkie-talkie right as she said it. "Wow!"

"Take yours to the other side of the library, and I'll stand by the door. Let's see if the reception reaches." He spun around and ran for the door.

Maria backed into the bookshelves in the far corner of the library. She heard static from her walkie-talkie and Sebastian's voice flowing through it.

"This is about the distance from me upstairs and you down below. How good is my reception?"

It took Maria a moment to process the enormity of

Sebastian's gift. This was no childish toy! This was a lifeline!

Maria pressed the button on her walkie-talkie and said, "Reception's good."

She met Sebastian in the middle of the library, unable to cover her smile. "Where did you get this?" she asked him.

"Oh, it was something I got a few years ago for my birthday. I knew it would come in handy someday."

Maria cradled the device in her hand like a prize, as if it were the buried treasure in Mrs. Fisher's apartment. Her eyes met Sebastian's. "Thanks. Really, thank you."

Sebastian smiled. "Now you *have* to let me help you find that treasure."

"Okay," she said in barely a whisper, pushing the toy deep inside her pocket. Then, with more confidence, she added, "I'll contact you as soon as I get another clue!"

"I'll be waiting for further instruction," said Sebastian, and gave her a salute.

"Maria! May I have a word with you?"

Maria spun around. Ms. Madigan had returned from her break. Maria's smile sank. She was so excited about the walkie-talkie, she'd forgotten to keep an eye out for the librarian. She glanced at the exit, but there was no way to speed out of there gracefully. Slowly, Maria nodded. "Sure," she said, but edged her way to the door.

"I researched your mother's nonprofit on that business

card, and I just wanted to know if everything is . . . okay at home." Ms. Madigan kept up with Maria as they moved.

Maria felt sick. She wanted to bolt, but she only responded, "Yes."

Ms. Madigan hesitated. "I know it is none of my business, but if your mother is in trouble, maybe we can help her look for quality work. The library has services—"

"No!" Maria said, and backed away. Ms. Madigan WAS onto her now. Her mother was right: Maria had exposed them to someone potentially dangerous.

"Yes, Maria, we can." Ms. Madigan reached out and held Maria's arm. "I can help her find legitimate employment."

Maria glared at Ms. Madigan's hand and kept moving toward the door. "No, Ms. Madigan. We don't need any help, thank you." She knew she had to get out of there before she said too much.

Ms. Madigan's grip tightened. "Maria, I'd like to help you."

Maria started to tremble. If she told Ms. Madigan everything, her mother would go to jail and Maria would be sent away to foster care. If she said nothing, then Maria would be moving away. Either way she would lose. But at least she would have SOMEONE if she moved with her mom. She looked directly into the librarian's worried eyes and tore away from her grip. "I have to go, Ms. Madigan!"

Maria pushed through the door to the library.

"Wait! Maria!" she heard the librarian call after her.

Maria ran several blocks before she realized she'd left her research back at the library. She slowly retraced her steps. That notebook carried all the evidence Ms. Madigan would need to prove that Madame Destine was a fraud. She sat on a stoop near the library so she could think. The toy in her pocket dug into her hip.

The toy!

She pulled out the walkie-talkie and pressed down hard on the button.

"Sebastian?" she said. "Are you there?"

She waited for five long seconds before static boomed from her toy. "You left me at the library!"

"Can you grab my notebook I left at my table? I'm just down the block."

"Sure thing, over and out."

Maria jumped up from the stoop and waited. Then she saw him: Sebastian clutching her notebook and racing to meet her. Maria couldn't help but smile and wave.

"Sebastian, have you ever been to the Strand? It's a bookstore."

"No," he said, "but I can look it up on my phone. Why?"

"Remember when the librarian was talking about hard-to-find books by the Beat poets? He said they were valuable?"

"Yeah," Sebastian said. "So what?"

"I'm just curious how valuable," she said. "You feel like coming with me to the city?

Sebastian looked at his phone and shrugged. "I still have a few hours before my mom wants me home."

"Let's go!" said Maria.

Maria and Sebastian got off the train at Union Square to a bustling sidewalk of pedestrian traffic. They turned right down Broadway and weaved through street crowds, until they stopped before carts containing used books. The building beside the carts displayed STRAND BOOKS on a red awning.

"This must be the place," said Maria, before pushing open the door to find herself in a store filled with people and a couple million books. "But where do we start?"

"I'll check upstairs," said Sebastian, trailing behind her. "Let me know what you find by walkie-talkie."

Maria nodded and turned the volume up on the plastic device. Then she weaved her way through the stacks. Most of the books appeared to be new, so she rushed to the basement for the used books. Fiction. Poetry. Psychology.

Suddenly her walkie-talkie buzzed. "Maria. It's on the third floor. Come on up!"

Five minutes later, Maria and Sebastian stood in the rare book room. It was much quieter and less busy than the main store. The spines of most of the books looked a lot older, too. There were even some behind glass.

A woman with slick black hair took off her glasses and smiled. "Are you two looking for something?"

Maria pursed her lips and tried to make her most serious face. "Yes. We were wondering what makes a book rare."

"Usually first editions of popular books. Age can be a factor, or even scarcity."

"What's the most valuable book you sell?" asked Sebastian before he sneezed.

The woman laughed. "Bless you!"

Sebastian sneezed again. "Sorry! I'm allergic to something in here."

"That's okay," the woman said. "To answer your question, I don't know, maybe James Joyce's *Ulysses*?"

"But how much does it sell for?" asked Maria a little impatient.

The clerk stood up and walked around the desk. "They range in price. Anywhere from ten dollars to a couple of thousand." Then she turned to Sebastian. "But *Ulysses* is priced at thirty-eight thousand dollars."

Sebastian's mouth fell open. "No way!"

"It's true," said the clerk, laughing. "Are you two interested in starting a collection of rare books? We have a first edition *Curious George* for around four thousand five hundred dollars."

Maria and Sebastian looked at each other with wide eyes. "No thank you," said Maria. "Do you have anything by Jack Kerouac that is . . . really rare?"

The clerk gave Maria a puzzled expression. "Maybe a first edition of *Dr. Sax*," she said. "It's only four hundred fifty dollars, so it's not super rare."

"Thank you," said Maria before turning to Sebastian. "The treasure isn't gold and silver hidden behind a painting."

"No?" said Sebastian.

"I think we're looking for the lost books of the Beat poets. With the price of that James Joyce book? the rarer the better."

Suddenly Maria thought about Mrs. Fisher's books in her apartment. If some of them were lost or missing, then Edward's riddle would make sense. They might even be worth money. And maybe one of them contained Beat poetry.

A day later, Maria found herself back at Mrs. Fisher's apartment with the widow shaking her head. "I'm sorry, Maria. You can go through my books, but I don't possess anything that could be that valuable."

Maria browsed through Mrs. Fisher's books anyway. "But it would make sense. Your husband's press, the missing Beat poet manuscripts."

Mrs. Fisher stroked Archimedes's fur. "My husband's printing press could have produced some of those works. He stored them in the basement years ago, but he told me he got rid of them when the publishing house folded, just before he died. He was so upset, we never talked about it again."

"Can we go down there and check?" asked Maria.

"Not without disturbing the tenants on the first floor. Besides, that was years ago!"

Maria hated being at a dead end. If it wasn't art and it wasn't rare books, then what else could the treasure be? She hated that Edward wouldn't just tell her where the treasure was.

The only thing she could do was wait for another clue.

16
The Getaway

A few days after visiting Mrs. Fisher, Maria lay on her bed with her notebook. She could feel the lump of the walkie-talkie hidden under her mattress. It reminded her of a fairy tale she'd read called "The Princess and the Pea," only in reverse. Here she was penniless but happy to sleep in discomfort. The lump was just a reminder she was no longer alone. She had Edward and Mrs. Fisher—and Sebastian, a kid her own age.

A frosty chill caused the hair to stand up on Maria's arm. Then she felt a tingling at the back of her neck.

"Edward?" Maria asked while she felt around her mattress for a pen. "Where've you been? I've been waiting to talk to you!" Maria lined herself up in position over the paper, her pen resting between her knuckles. "Okay, Edward. Talk to me."

*　*　*

After ten minutes, Maria opened her eyes and shook her head. She was groggy, but in front of her was a message written in beautiful script:

The blank canvas is the hardest for the artist to harness.
But false starts and mess-ups are part of the process.
Go over this subject with one last detail:
I was his student that failed when I fell.
Tell Mrs. Fisher I miss her, and she'll get the picture.

Maria studied the paper. "Who was your teacher, Edward? So, you *do* know Mrs. Fisher! Is that how you knew she had gingersnaps?" Maria fumbled for the pen and waited in her usual position for Edward to guide her. But the air was no longer cool.

Maria glanced at the lump in her mattress. She should tell Sebastian about the clue. Although she'd fantasized about contacting her friend on the walkie-talkie, she worried that her mother would discover it. She would have to be quiet if she wanted to talk to Sebastian without arousing suspicion.

Maria pushed her hand under her mattress and brought out her walkie-talkie. She pressed the button and whispered, "Sebastian! Do you read me?"

Maria threw the walkie-talkie on her bed and stared at it.

A few seconds later, Sebastian responded. "I'm here, over." Maria grabbed the toy and turned the volume down so that it was barely audible.

"I got another clue," she whispered. "We are really close!"

"Can you read it to me?"

Maria read the first line of the poem, and Sebastian repeated it. "The bank cactus is the hardest or the farthest?"

"No," Maria said. "Let me read it again. The blank canvas—"

"The bank and us— Why are you whispering?"

"No!" Maria said. "Listen. The blank—"

"Why don't you just bring it up to me?" said Sebastian.

Maria debated whether it would be easier to sneak out and hand over the clue to Sebastian, or if she should continue trying to whisper the note over walkie-talkie. If she could sneak out without her mother knowing, then yes, she could see Sebastian. But if her mother was still home, there was not a chance that she would even attempt to see her friend. Maria knew she was on dangerously thin ice with her mom and Mr. Fox.

Maria wanted to see Sebastian. She wanted to hand him the note and see his gap-toothed grin, even if it was only for a second. Maybe through this small gesture of passing a note, the ice would crack, and she would be in more trouble than she had ever known before. But Maria couldn't hide in her closet for the rest of her life and hope that life would find her.

"I'll see if I can make a getaway," said Maria. "Over and out." She turned off her walkie-talkie so that it wouldn't make a noise while she was away, and stuffed it back under her mattress.

※ ※ ※

Maria tiptoed carefully over the old floorboards in her mother's bedroom.

CREEEEEEAK.

She stopped, hoping that the noise hadn't been heard.

"Is that you, Maria?" Madame Destine called from the kitchen.

Maria's hopes hit the floor. She wouldn't be going anywhere tonight. "Yes! I was just looking for you!" she said, trying not to sound disappointed.

"We're in here."

Maria dragged her feet into the kitchen to find Madame Destine and Mr. Fox with their noses buried in the newspaper like two lions crouched in high grass.

"This one!" said Mr. Fox, swiping up a pen and circling

a listing in red. "White van, fair condition. Twenty thousand miles. Asking price four thousand dollars." He jerked his head up and waited for Madame Destine's approval.

"Maybe," she said, and nodded. "Just maybe."

Houdini turned his beak and glanced at Maria.

"Why are you looking for vans?" asked Maria.

"Ahhh," said Madame Destine, pulling her head away from the paper. "There's my little Miss Motormouth. Good question! Sit down!"

Maria dropped to her chair at the table and gripped her knees.

"We're running dangerously low on cash. Fox and I are looking for a van. More specifically, a *getaway* van."

"GETAWAY VAN," echoed Houdini.

Mr. Fox took out his cell phone. "Should I dial the number?"

Houdini, perching on Madame Destine's shoulder, rustled his feathers while she nodded. Then she rose from the table and began pacing the kitchen. "We have just enough money left to buy our ticket outta town."

"Oh," replied Maria. She tried to give off the appearance of indifference, but inside she was screaming. They were really going to leave.

"But absolutely nothing remains for living expenses while we relocate," continued Madame Destine, her words sounding calculating and cold.

"Oh, I see," said Maria. She tried to picture them in another town, having to start over at a new library and make up new lies to tell people. It would always be this way, no matter where they lived. She'd always be hiding. It was pointless starting over now. "Then maybe we should just stay where we are," she mumbled.

"Not a chance," said Madame Destine, like a harsh slap. She crept around the table and stood behind Maria's chair. Then she ran her fingers through Maria's hair, as if to comb it. "I know we've had our ups and downs lately, Maria . . ."

Maria thought, YOU CAN SAY THAT AGAIN, but tried to give the impression that she was unaware of there being a problem. Her mother's nails felt good against her scalp. They were gentle and soothing.

"But I have just a teensy-weensy favor to ask you," continued Madame Destine.

A catch! Of course there was a catch. What could her mother possibly want from her, and did she really have any choice in the matter? Maria's scalp tingled, making it difficult to think clearly. She mustered a shrug. "What?"

"We'll need to make one more con before we skip town," said Madame Destine. Her heavy hands dropped suddenly to Maria's shoulders. "I was wondering if I could count on my girl to be so kind as to assist me." Madame Destine's cold fingers wrapped around Maria's neck. "Without messing it up," she added, pressing her fingernails into Maria's skin. "And without telling a single person!" Maria could feel the blood draining from her ears, and she began to tremble. Finally, her mother released her grip. "I would be so grateful!"

Maria gasped. Beads of sweat rolled off her forehead, and a chilling fear swept over her. "Wha-what do I have to do?"

"Just do what I tell you when the time comes," Madame Destine said, and returned to her chair at the table.

"It's ringing," said Mr. Fox. "Everyone shut up." After a few moments, Mr. Fox said, "Yes, I'm interested in taking a look at your van. When would you be available?"

Maria tried to breathe slowly. They were going to leave, and there was nothing she could do about it.

"Why, er, yes. I guess I'm available today. Is someone else interested? Got it. I'll swing by with the missus within the hour. Yes, we'll be paying in cash . . . What's the addy?" Mr. Fox grabbed a sheet of Maria's copy paper and her pen from the fruit bowl. Then he scribbled down the address. "Very good. We're on our way." Mr. Fox dropped the phone on the table before shifting his eyes to Madame Destine. "We gotta go. Now. Someone else is interested and is looking first thing tomorrow."

"Now?" asked Madame Destine, examining her outfit. She pushed open the door to her bedroom and said, "Okay, let me get ready." Madame Destine rushed into her room and saw her reflection in her vanity mirror. She adjusted her turban, pushing a thin strand of hair back under.

Maria watched from the kitchen, trying to suppress her smile. She would have the place to herself!

"No time," said Mr. Fox, swiping his wallet and phone from the kitchen table. "We gotta boogie to Harlem. It's an hour by train. Let's go!"

Madame Destine swiped a tube of lipstick from her drawer and applied it slowly. Her eyes met Maria's in the mirror, and she cleared her throat. "I'm gonna TRUST you to stay outta trouble while I'm gone. Do you hear me?"

Maria nodded, but secretly, she couldn't believe her luck! "I won't step away from this building," she said, and she meant it. She would just be upstairs with Sebastian.

Maria followed them to the front parlor where Madame Destine placed Houdini in his cage. She bent her face to the bars and baby talked, "Mommy will be back shortly, my precious." She kissed Houdini's feathered forehead through the cage before shutting the door.

Madame Destine and Mr. Fox rushed to the door. But just as they walked out, Madame Destine turned and raised a brow. "And I mean it. Don't disobey me," she said, her eyes probing Maria.

"Of course not," Maria said.

Madame Destine and Mr. Fox slammed the door behind them.

Maria froze in the hallway and counted to fifty. Then she took a deep breath and smiled. She'd just won bingo. Her prize? Freedom to see Sebastian.

She cracked the front door and escaped into the night as light as an autumn breeze.

17
A Home-Cooked Meal

Maria had to climb the stairs above her garden apartment to get to Sebastian's. Even though they technically lived in the same building and there was originally a way to get into his apartment through her kitchen, the entrance had long been sealed off. Maria rang Sebastian's buzzer.

She felt a mix of fear and excitement standing on his doorstep. She never imagined that she'd be bold enough to *visit* a neighbor—and just a few feet from her own home. She scanned the street behind her just in case Mr. Fox and her mother had decided to return, but the street was empty. Maria shivered. She was suddenly overcome with fear of meeting Sebastian's family. She almost turned away but—

Footsteps hit the stairs inside Sebastian's apartment and the shadow of a head darted across the curtains in the window. Then the handle jiggled before the door swung open.

"Hi there," said a slim woman with brown skin and a head full of puffy hair. She was beautiful.

"Are you here to see Sebastian?" the woman asked, and ushered Maria in. "I'm Sebastian's mom, Mrs. Goldstein, but you can call me Shanya."

"I'm Maria," Maria mumbled. "I live downstairs." She met Mrs. Goldstein's eyes and quickly looked away.

"Of course!" replied Sebastian's mother. She gave a warm smile to Maria.

Sebastian stood at the top of the stairs holding his walkie-talkie. "Come on up!" he called to Maria.

"I'm just cooking lasagna," said Mrs. Goldstein. "Will you be staying for dinner?"

Maria didn't know what to say. She hadn't thought about how long she could stay while her mother was away. And what was the thing Sebastian's mom said she was cooking?

"Yes, Mom, she's staying for dinner," Sebastian shouted above them. Then he motioned to Maria. "Come up. We have work to do!"

Like a racer that has just heard the sound of the gun, Maria shot up the long flight of stairs to meet Sebastian. When she reached the top, she breathlessly took in the bright space. She was pretty sure Sebastian's family lived with every light on in the house. The whole place smelled clean, and the wooden floors twinkled with varnish. The walls had been freshly painted, and a family portrait hung in the hallway.

Maria took a closer look at the photo. Sebastian was standing in front of his beautiful mother. A pale man stood behind them like a sea captain. He had a rippled forehead and a turbulent wave of hair above thick-framed glasses.

"Where's your dad?" asked Maria.

"He's working, but he'll be home for dinner," Sebastian said. "Follow me." He grabbed Maria by the hand and pulled her down the hall to his bedroom. As soon as they entered, Sebastian shut the door and whispered, "Show me the clue."

Maria dug in her pocket and pulled out the wrinkled message and waved it at him.

"Where did you get this?" Sebastian said. He grabbed it and dropped to the edge of his bed, where he hovered over the words.

Maria gave a slight shrug before she took in Sebastian's bedroom. His walls were painted a light blue, like a spring sky, but the ceiling was black and splattered with hundreds of glow-in-the-dark stars. A yellow-painted basketball dangled above Sebastian's bed. It resembled the sun. Not far from it was a baseball painted red with rings of purple pipe cleaners that Maria guessed was supposed to be Saturn.

There was a bulletin board by the door filled with first place ribbons. Trophies lined the shelves of his dresser.

But more impressive was Sebastian's window! Maria took a peek outside. The tops of the trees and high-rises poked above the brownstones. Maria couldn't believe it.

It was such a different view from her garden apartment. Sebastian had a whole window in his room, not just a vent in the closet to spy through!

"So the other poem was about poets and artists, right?" asked Sebastian. He took off his cap and massaged his head. "This must be something else to do with them."

Maria shrugged. "Maybe. I don't know," she said, falling onto the bed next to him. The two stared at the words for a long time. Maria could smell the aroma of baked lasagna and melted cheese. A long growl came from her stomach. "You have a nice room," she said to cover up the noise.

"Uh . . . thanks."

"Nice planets." Maria smiled and glanced up.

Sebastian grinned. "I like science. A lot. It's my favorite subject. Especially astronomy. Black holes, wormholes, stuff like that."

"What are those ribbons for?" she asked, and pointed to his bulletin board.

"Oh, they're nothing." Sebastian leaned back on one arm. "My dad likes them. He's kind of into me winning ribbons."

"Are they from school?" Maria was very curious about what it would be like to attend school, surrounded by other students. She wondered if all students got ribbons or if Sebastian was special.

"I won the spelling bee three years in a row at my old school. Another ribbon is for the science fair, and another is for never missing a day of school. I didn't get sick once while I was in third grade." Sebastian grinned. "Notice how none of my ribbons and trophies are in sports?" Sebastian sighed. "You've seen me try to catch and throw a ball."

Maria couldn't help but smile. She was impressed. She wondered what kind of student she would be if her mother let her to go to school.

"You don't win trophies when you're homeschooled," she said softly, and began to fidget with Sebastian's bed-spread. His blanket had vibrant stripes, and the fabric was soft, so unlike the thin gray blanket she slept under.

"But you're lucky," Sebastian said. "I wish I could stay home and read whatever I wanted! I would read up on just science if I could."

Maria leaned back, making herself more comfortable. "It's not exactly like that. I enjoy science, and I love read-ing stories, too. But I can't read JUST what I want to all day."

"I guess reading stories is okay," admitted Sebastian. "Especially the true ones."

"Like what?" she asked. She rarely read any nonfiction, except her mother's obituaries, of course. She preferred read-ing fantasies by authors like Lois Lowry, Madeleine L'Engle, and Roald Dahl.

"I like reading about real people," said Sebastian." You know, how they lived and what they did." Then he pointed to his ceiling. "One day I'll explore a planet."

Maria was surprised at how sure Sebastian sounded when he said it. It had never occurred to her to plan so far into the future, because she'd never thought much further than her mother's next con.

"What do you want to be?" asked Sebastian. "You know, when you grow up."

Maria pictured herself as an adult in Madame Destine's clothes—a heavy turban and a guilty conscience weighing her down. She knew her mother cared for her, and that was why she had taught her everything she knew about conning. But was it enough? Was Maria ungrateful for desiring something more? She may not have had a window that looked out into the world, but she had a peephole illuminating her mother's schemes, something that was needed to survive in this world.

"I want to be rich," said Maria, thinking about all the times her mother told her that was what she should want. But deep down, Maria knew that wasn't really what she wanted. Sure, she had Edward and this talent for "automatic writing," but would that make her rich? Was there some secret to a happy life that was better than gold and jewels?

Sebastian sighed. "Then you should talk to my dad. He's always looking for ways to make more money."

Maria held up the clue. "It says that he was a student in the message. And he knew Mrs. Fisher while he was alive. Could Mr. Fisher have been Edward's teacher?"

Sebastian shrugged. "I don't know. You're the one who's talked to her."

The front door jiggled open downstairs, and a muffled, deep voice said, "Hey, Shanya! Smells like lasagna."

"Dad's home," said Sebastian.

They were interrupted by a knock on Sebastian's door. His mom poked her head through the opening.

"Dinner's ready, you two. Wash up and come to the table."

Maria held the fork in her hand and stabbed at the steaming lasagna on her plate. The gooey cheese and pasta had strange ingredients inside of it that Maria had never seen. Were these vegetables? She glanced at Sebastian for clues on how to eat this meal. He held his knife in his left hand as he sawed the pasta into segments while holding the operation steady with the fork in his right hand. Maria thought that she could manage this.

"Does your mother cook, Maria?" asked Mrs. Goldstein.

"She doesn't have time," replied Maria.

"Yeah, she's pretty busy," said Sebastian. "Not only is she a psychic but she also runs a nonprofit, right, Maria?"

Maria quickly stuffed a huge helping of lasagna in her mouth so that she could think up an answer, but the hot food burned, and a string of cheese rested on her chin. Her face flushed red with embarrassment.

"Let her eat, Sebastian!" said his mother. "Maria, enjoy your food!"

After a few minutes, Mr. Goldstein cleared his throat. "How long have you and your mother lived in your apartment?" he asked.

Maria shrugged. "My whole life, I guess," she mumbled.

"I bet they got their place for a steal before the neighborhood blew up," Mr. Goldstein told his wife. Sebastian's dad looked burdened and serious, like he didn't know the meaning of the word *fun*. Sebastian's mom, on the other hand, looked like she'd invented the word. She dressed in colorful clothing that made her seem like a movie star.

Mrs. Goldstein shook her head. "You know, I read my horoscopes, Maria, but I've never considered getting advice from a psychic. I've been meaning to consult with your mother, but I get spooked out by that stuff sometimes!" She laughed and took a sip of water. "I bet you get some interesting visitors!"

Maria swallowed her food. "Mostly widows," she said.

"Where do you go to school?" asked Sebastian's father.

"She's homeschooled, Dad!" Sebastian said before reaching for his milk.

"Wow, your mother *must* be busy, then," said Sebastian's mom. "If she's also a teacher, then she has her work cut out for her! It's hard for me just to remember which keys I need to bring when I meet with my clients."

Maria's leg bobbed up and down in her chair. Had she known that she was going to be bombarded with questions, she would never have stayed for dinner. Sebastian's parents were like Ms. Madigan. Too many questions. And what was this stuff she was eating? It was hot, and the texture was soft and different from the beef jerky and chips her mother served her. It wasn't *bad*, but it took some getting used to. She knew that she definitely did not belong here. This was a family where the mother cooked hot dinners with exotic ingredients. Their kid was an overachiever in school, and the dad wore a suit to work and talked about money. No fists banged on the table. None of them screamed at each other.

"Maria, what are you and your mom studying right now?" asked Sebastian's mother.

Maria thought of the public records she read along with the obituaries and society pages in the newspaper. "Current affairs," she said.

"Really!" Sebastian's mother exclaimed. "I can barely keep up with the news, let alone try to teach it." Mrs. Goldstein laughed.

"I got an A on the science quiz," said Sebastian.

"Very good," said Mr. Goldstein. "But next time shoot for the stars. I want to see A pluses!" Mr. Goldstein winked at Sebastian.

"Oh, Alex," said Sebastian's mom. "He's doing just fine in school!" She turned to Sebastian. "I'm so proud of you!"

"It's a parent's job to encourage, Shanya." Mr. Goldstein pointed his fork at Sebastian. "If he shoots for the stars, he'll get there!" Mr. Goldstein brought his vibrating phone up to the table. "It's work," he said, and grimaced.

"Do you have to take it?" asked Mrs. Goldstein. "We're having dinner, and we have a guest."

"It will *just* be a minute. I promise." Mr. Goldstein leaned in to kiss his wife before he shot into the kitchen to answer his work call.

Maria couldn't believe it. Sebastian's father just kissed his mother. She never saw Madame Destine kiss Mr. Fox.

"Oh, Maria. We are usually not this rude." Mrs. Goldstein sighed. "But Alex has been under a lot of stress with work. I hope you understand."

Maria fumbled with a cherry tomato that had rolled away from her salad. "We answer calls at the table all the time," she mumbled. "And make them, too."

"Oh, really?" said Sebastian's mom, and refilled her glass of water from the pitcher. "Your mom's very busy!"

Was her mom busy? Mostly she would lie around and let Maria do the work. Maria smiled nervously.

"What's for dessert, Mom?" Sebastian grinned at Maria. "IF you're lucky, it will be Mom's chocolate cake."

"It's a surprise," said his mom, her face beaming with pride. "Let's wait until Maria finishes," said Mrs. Goldstein, picking up her plate. "I whipped it up last week for my clients when we were closing on a three-bedroom. I thought I'd make it for us this week."

Maria tried to wrap the cheese around the fork, but as soon as she put it in her mouth, it was on her chin again. She wiped her face with her napkin and placed it carefully back in her lap, as Sebastian did. She felt like an alien visiting Earth for the first time.

"I'm pretty full, but I could make some room for dessert," Maria said.

"Sweetie, you barely ate your lasagna. I don't want your mother getting mad at me for only serving you junk food."

Maria was confused. She was definitely from another planet in this home. Just a few floors below, Maria's family ate ice cream for dinner.

She scooped a large forkful of pasta into her mouth and swallowed.

"Whoa, there! You must really want dessert!" said Mrs. Goldstein. She hopped up from her chair and laughed. "And now, my two plate cleaners, I'll be back with your surprise!" Sebastian's mom swept up their plates and disappeared into the kitchen.

"I hope it's crème brûlée!" said Sebastian.

Crème brûlée? Maria had no idea what he was talking about, but the lasagna rested like a lump in her stomach.

How could she keep sitting there making a fool of herself? Sebastian's family seemed to have it all: money, happiness, a nice apartment. And Maria? She had nothing. Barely a family. Maria felt like a rat; sooner or later they'd realize she was not one of them and send her back down to the gutter.

But she wanted so badly to *stay.*

Maria felt her throat close up. Was it wrong to want Sebastian's life?

"Or maybe Mom has made a pie," Sebastian said. "Blueberry is my favorite. What's yours?"

Maria's eyes moistened. She had never had a real pie before, one that was home-cooked. Maria couldn't understand why Madame Destine could con her way into hard cash but couldn't fake her way into happiness. Maria wanted a mother who encouraged her to succeed at whatever she wished. She wanted a room with a window, freshly painted walls, family portraits—and a kiss on the cheek. Maria wanted a mother she felt *close* to.

Then Maria knew what she was missing. She didn't care if she was rich or if she ever found treasure. What she wanted more than anything was a home. A *real* home, with a family that cared about her and loved her.

Sebastian's mother entered the dining room with a large bowl of vanilla wafers peeking out from behind a fluffy cloud of yellow. "Voila!" she exclaimed. "Banana pudding!"

But Maria had already jumped up and backed away from the table. She *had* to leave. It was as if she had gotten a taste of something that was too good for her, and she was afraid of it. She knew where she belonged: downstairs, hidden in the shadows with con artists and stale air.

"Thank you for everything, but I have to go home," Maria said before she turned around and fled down the bright hall. She descended the long flight of stairs and shot through the front door into the cold night.

18
Signs for the Searchers

Maria woke to her mother's voice outside the door of her closet. She rubbed her eyes and sighed. It would be so much easier to just lie there and shut out the world. There she could hide under heavy coats in her tiny room, the crack of light under the door the only reminder of life happening around her—the life she never wanted.

She peeled herself from her mattress with great effort. Maria felt worse than a piece of taffy stuck to its wrapper. She cracked the door of the closet, just missing Madame Destine, who zipped past her into the kitchen. Maria took a deep breath and followed her.

"You overslept."

Maria shrugged as she slid around her mother and filled up an empty Styrofoam cup with soda. It was infuriating that Mr. Fox had packed all their dinnerware in boxes already.

"It's time to start pulling your own weight around here," he said, and jotted something down on Maria's paper with her pen.

"What more can I do?"

"I'm glad you asked!" Madame Destine said with a slap on Maria's back. "While we drove the van back last night, John and I discussed how we should make our last con in New York City." Madame Destine fed Houdini some bread crumbs from the table.

"LAST CON!" echoed Houdini.

"But seeing how the FBI is onto us, we must be extra careful."

Maria rolled her eyes. Now it was the FBI, no longer the police. Her mother was paranoid!

"So Fox and I have a plan."

"Aye, we do, my dear," joined in Mr. Fox, his grin a deep scar across his face.

"You've been so helpful finding all of these widows, Maria, but we've decided to expand our audience AND play it safe this time." Madame Destine pulled up a chair and pressed Maria down so that she landed in it with a thud. "People are so very gullible. Everyone feels pain. Everyone looks for answers. That's all anybody wants: answers to ease their pain."

Maria opened a package of Twinkies and tried to scoop out the white cream from the yellow cake. If only it were a baguette from Mrs. Fisher's apartment.

"And that's where we come in," added Mr. Fox as he swiped a pair of scissors from the counter and sliced through the paper.

"John is making flyers," said Madame Destine. "Flyers for the lonely. Flyers for the lost. Flyers for those looking for answers as they roam the cold, hard streets in this godforsaken town!" Madame Destine threw up her arms, causing her parrot to fly about.

"But, Mom," Maria said, "how are random flyers going to land us enough money to leave?" She swallowed the yellow shell of the cake and washed it down with a swig of soda.

"My sweet child. We may be down on our funds, but we've got your paper. We've got your pens. And we have a VAN."

"So?" asked Maria.

"That's all we need to spread the word!" sang Madame Destine. "We're driving this van all over the city, and we're posting our flyers on electrical poles and fences!"

Maria only now took in the stack of paper cut into thin strips with Mr. Fox's penmanship scrawled across them. She pulled one from the top of the stack and read the message:

PSYCHIC

FEELING LOST? LOOKING FOR ANSWERS?
THE GREAT MADAME DESTINE HAS THEM 4 U!

"But aren't you afraid of attracting the FBI?" asked Maria. "I thought we were going for widows instead of having a bunch of strangers in our place."

"Too much research!" said Madame Destine with a wave of her hand. "Besides, we can tell them whatever we want."

"But how many people do you think will respond from a random flyer posted?" asked Maria.

Mr. Fox growled, "Don't question your mother!" He threw the scissors down and bent close to Madame Destine's ear. "She's cruisin' for a bruisin'."

Madame Destine shushed Mr. Fox and focused on her daughter. "No, no, Maria. I'm SO glad you asked." She swooped her arm around her and continued in a gentle tone. "You see, YOU are not lost. Nor are you looking for answers. People pass flyers every day; that is true!" Madame Destine straightened her posture and snatched an ad from the stack. "It's only when people are *looking* for something that they finally *SEE* something." Madame Destine held the flyer in front of her before she nuzzled Houdini with a kiss. "And that's where we come in. Only people who are searching will see our flyers. No one else will pay any mind. And they're willing to pay good money to *believe*. We're not doing ANYTHING wrong! It's legal, and it's called entertainment."

"Yeah," said Mr. Fox. "For once we're legit."

"Now what I need from you is to stay home and finish packing. But leave the parlor alone. We'll be using that room until we hit the road." Madame Destine rubbed her hands over Maria's hair, flattening her curls. "If anyone shows up, don't answer the door." She gave Maria a stern look. "I don't want snoops when I'm not around."

Mr. Fox swooped up the rest of Maria's paper, now filled with advertisements. "I'm ready when you are, Destine."

"You got the tape?" asked Maria's mother.

"It's in the van."

Madame Destine stomped to the front of the apartment. Maria heard Houdini's cage door creak open and slam shut. "And, Maria," said her mother, "do NOT fail me!"

The front door crashed shut and echoed across the apartment, followed by the screeching of tires and the heavy moan of a van pulling away.

Maria glanced around the apartment and made a mental list:

1. Her mother's bedroom needed to be packed.
2. Her coats needed to be boxed and labeled.
3. The bathroom needed to be organized to just the essentials.

This would take her most of the day. Maria took several

shallow breaths, feeling overwhelmed. She needed to see Mrs. Fisher to find out if her husband had been Edward's teacher. If that was the case, they may very well be close to finding the treasure!

If she didn't find the treasure, she'd be failing Edward.

And she'd also be leaving Sebastian.

Maria longed to connect with her friends just once more before she left the only world she'd ever known. Soon she'd be in an even lonelier world of getaway vans, highways, and her mother's delusion of being followed by the FBI.

She opened the door to her mother's closet and punched the heavy coats. The coats rocked back, causing one to fall from a hanger and land on Maria's bed. She reached for the coat but stopped at the small lump in her mattress. She could call Sebastian! Of course!

For once she would ask someone for help.

19
Message Received

Maria screamed into her walkie-talkie, "Sebastian! Can you hear me?" She turned up the volume. "Are you there, Sebastian?" She waited, staring into the face of the plastic T. rex. Maria bolted out of her bedroom, brushing past her mother's newspaper clippings. Her palm sweated while holding the walkie-talkie as she took inventory of the boxes in the kitchen.

"I read you," replied the dinosaur underneath a blanket of static.

Maria felt a smile stretch from ear to ear. "Sebastian! I need your help. Can you come downstairs?" She waited long enough to watch a fly land on the empty fruit bowl.

"I'll be right there," replied the fuzzy voice from the toy.

Maria carefully turned off her walkie-talkie and hid it back under her mattress. Then she sprinted down the hallway, sliding in her socks until she reached the front door. The door slammed from the apartment upstairs, and Sebastian descended the stone stairs.

Before he could knock, Maria swung open the door. "Come in," she said, pulling him inside.

Sebastian entered with some hesitation, taking in his surroundings as if he were entering a haunted house.

"I need you to help me pack," said Maria. "And don't ask questions!"

Sebastian's mouth fell open. "Are you moving?"

"There's no time. I'll explain later." Maria handed Sebastian a box. His large, unblinking eyes took everything in.

"Follow me," Maria ordered. She dragged him into the kitchen and pulled open the pantry and cupboards. "Clear all this out into the box."

"But—"

"Later! There isn't time."

Sebastian grabbed Maria's arm. "You have a lot of explaining to do!"

"EXPLAINING!" squawked a voice in the other room.

Sebastian let go and jumped. "Was that your mother?"

"It's just her parrot," replied Maria, before she swooped her arm through the pantry, knocking junk food into a box already full of beef jerky, chips, and cookies. But a slight smile appeared that she couldn't suppress. She was relieved that even Sebastian thought that parrot was creepy.

Sebastian turned his hat around and began to work, taping up a box. But then he stopped. "Why are we packing junk food?"

Maria shrugged before she shut the box and labeled it FOOD in black Sharpie.

After they were done in the kitchen, Maria handed Sebastian another box and dragged him into her mother's bedroom. She flung open the closet door and pointed at her mother's collection of coats. "Fill the boxes with these furs," she ordered.

Sebastian dropped the box to the floor and pointed at Maria's bed. "Someone sleeps here?"

Maria carefully ignored him and disappeared into the kitchen. She returned with a trash bag. Then she ripped each and every obituary from the wall of her mother's bedroom.

The wall was white under the clippings, not a dull mustard like the rest of the apartment.

Sebastian sneezed in the closet. There was a harsh screech of hangers across the bar. "I'm allergic to dust mites," he said.

Maria crumpled the obituary clippings and wiped the dust off her fingers. She glanced at the benevolent face of her grandmother on the faded poster and carefully pried off the tacks holding it in place. The poster smelled old, like Mrs. Fisher's home. She shut her eyes and took in the scent of Mrs. Fisher. She knew if they hurried, they could make it there and back before her mother and Mr. Fox returned.

Sebastian might even cut her time in half, if he did what he was told and didn't ask questions.

Maria taped the rolled-up poster to keep it in place. Then she swung around to find Sebastian lugging the heavy box of coats from the closet.

"What do you want me to do with the mattress and blanket in the closet?"

"Leave it for now," replied Maria as she took the box from Sebastian and brought it into the kitchen.

"Maria?" Sebastian asked in a timid voice, following her into the kitchen. "Maria, where is your bedroom?"

Maria ignored him and filled a Styrofoam cup with water. Then she took a swig to buy herself some time before answering. She knew better than to tell him the truth about where she slept. After she'd seen his room, it would make him uncomfortable to see how she lived. Maria had to change the subject. "We have to get everything packed so I can take you to the treasure. You still want to find it, don't you?"

"Yes, but WHAT IS GOING ON HERE?" Sebastian said. "Why are we packing? Are you moving? And where are your pa—"

"There isn't time," Maria said.

When the boxes were neatly stacked in the kitchen, Maria slipped on her shoes. "You have your MetroCard?" she asked.

"Yes," answered Sebastian, "but where are we going?"

Maria pulled him through her apartment to the front door. Then she pushed her friend from her dark cave into the lively afternoon of the outside world.

"I'll race you to the train!" Maria said before she pushed the gate wide open and shot out.

Sebastian took a step through the gate and paused. Then he shook his head and said, "Wait for me!"

They flew down the sidewalk, dodging dog walkers and kids at play.

Maria's heart beat rapidly, like a tiny bird that had just been set free.

※　※　※

"The blank canvas is the hardest for the artist to harness," read Mrs. Fisher. She paused in front of the window in her living room and cleared her throat. "But false starts and mess-ups are part of the process . . ."

Maria gave Sebastian a sideways glance on the sofa and smiled. Then she took her last bite of the sandwich Mrs. Fisher had prepared for lunch. That afternoon, the widow had performed a few of her songs on the piano before she'd spun some of her favorite records. Albums by John Coltrane, Miles Davis, and Donald Byrd were strewn about the floor with her sheet music. Maria had suddenly remembered to give Mrs. Fisher the poem, and to her disappointment, the widow was stumped.

"I was his student that failed when I fell," continued Mrs. Fisher, her eyes glued to the message. "I was his student . . ." she mumbled. "Student." Mrs. Fisher paced back and forth in front of the window, stepping over a Billie Holiday record.

Sebastian bent down to pet Archimedes, but the cat darted back behind the sofa.

Maria waited for Mrs. Fisher to stop pacing. She'd felt the cold tingling of Edward's presence all afternoon but didn't want to tell Sebastian about him. If only Edward could have just TOLD them where the treasure was! These riddles and poems were driving her bonkers. She hoped with all her heart that this letter would jog Mrs. Fisher's memory so she could solve the riddle of who Edward really was once and for all.

"Now . . . Edward. Edward," said Mrs. Fisher to herself. "My memory must be failing me. My husband had a lot of students."

Archimedes peeked his head out from behind the sofa and nudged Sebastian's hand. But Sebastian had given up on petting the cat.

Maria snapped her fingers until she had the cat's attention, then she scooped him in her arms and cradled Archimedes as if he were a baby. She stood up with him and meandered across the living room to the mirror where she could admire her reflection with him again.

Inside the full-length mirror was an eleven-year-old girl

with a feisty cat . . . and just behind her were two friends. If Maria could freeze this moment in time, she would, because in that reflection, at that precise moment, was a snapshot of everything that made her feel happy. The afternoon sun beamed through the window and fell across the room like a warm blanket.

Oh! If only this moment would last!

But then the glow in the room faded, and Maria abruptly turned from the mirror. An icy chill shot down her back, and she dropped the cat. "Edward!" Maria called. He must have been losing his patience with her, she thought.

Mrs. Fisher stopped pacing. Both the widow and Sebastian stared at Maria.

Maria shivered, rubbing her arms as Archimedes darted behind the curtains.

Sebastian pushed his glasses up. "Who's Edward?"

"Yes," Mrs. Fisher added. "Who IS Edward?" She breezed past the sofa and stood beside Maria before turning to Sebastian. "I apologize, Sebastian. Have you been informed about Maria's friend Edward?" Then Mrs. Fisher gave Maria a nudge. "Do you want to tell him about your *friend*?"

Maria shook her head quickly.

"Is he here right now?" Mrs. Fisher asked.

Maria nodded. She knew she hadn't much time. IF she wanted to find the treasure and Edward's true identity, she needed to talk to him right then and there. So what if Sebastian would find out her secret? Mrs. Fisher knew. And if Sebastian didn't like it, well, she wouldn't be in New York City much longer anyway. She searched Sebastian's eager face. He stared at her unblinking, mouth open, with that gap tooth of his peeking out. Maybe he could be trusted.

"Can you pass me a pen and paper?" she asked.

"Certainly," responded the widow. She searched around on her dining room table for a pen. "Now, Sebastian, what you are about to see Maria do is very special. We like to call it *automatic writing*. It's when the spirit world sends messages through writing from the subconscious, and often it appears as poetry."

Sebastian adjusted his cap. "I don't understand. What does this have to do with . . . Edward and the treasure?"

Maria ignored him and pulled out a chair from the table. After the paper was in place, she sat at the table and balanced the pen between her knuckles. She shut her eyes and let her head fall back. The cool air consumed her while her hand rocked back and forth over the paper.

Sebastian gasped. "What's happening?"

"Shhhhh!" said Mrs. Fisher. "Let her finish."

* * *

Maria opened her eyes. The paper was no longer in front of her.

Sebastian shook his head, backing away from her chair. "What did you just do?"

Maria shivered. "Edward's a ghost," she said in a half yawn. Sebastian froze. It was hard for Maria to tell the expression on her friend's face. For what seemed like eternity, his mouth remained open, and his eyes grew large.

Finally, he took a deep breath. "Maria. Ghosts aren't real. There's no scientific proof."

Maria narrowed her eyes, trying to hold back her anger.

"But what you did was a cool trick! You'll have to teach—"

"I've got it!" said Mrs. Fisher. She dropped the paper to the floor and whisked down the hall. After a few moments, her voice sang, "Bingo! I found him!"

Maria and Sebastian raced through the living room and joined Mrs. Fisher in the hallway.

"It's Eddy De la Cruz!" she said. She pulled a framed photo from the wall and brought it close to Maria and Sebastian so they could see. The black-and-white photo showed a younger Mrs. Fisher laughing at a table with a balding man, presumably her late husband. They were surrounded by a crowd at the dinner party. "There!" Mrs. Fisher's nail tapped the glass surface of the photo. Her finger rested on the young face of a dark-haired man standing next to a young woman with dark features. He had a brooding brow joined by two creases. "This is your ghost!"

Maria took in the photo. So this was Edward. His dark looks made him sort of handsome, but he seemed quiet, tucked off to the side. She gave the photo back to Mrs. Fisher and asked, "But who *was* he?"

"He was one of my husband's students in the eighties!" Mrs. Fisher said, and beamed. "Such a sweet young man! He was a poet, and for a while he was a regular in this house. I last recall he married and had a family . . . but then I think his wife died. Oh, goodness, it's been so long. Poor Eddy!"

A poet? Maybe that explained all of the riddles and poems he'd sent her. But Maria wondered why Eddy had picked *her* to write through.

"That explains how he knew about the gingersnaps in the kitchen," Mrs. Fisher said. "He loved those cookies."

Sebastian shifted his weight beside Maria. "Let me get this straight. You both think this man's a ghost that's been talking to Maria. I don't buy it." Sebastian leaned against the wall.

Maria and Mrs. Fisher glanced at each other.

"I was told there was a treasure hidden in this apartment. Is this whole thing a joke?"

Maria made fists at her side. How could he think she was making all this up? She took a deep breath and tried to hold back from saying anything. Then she realized he did have a point. She had no idea what Eddy De la Cruz had to do with finding the treasure. Maybe Edward had made it all up. But why?

The light from the living room faded to a cool blue and

darkened the hallway where they stood. Mrs. Fisher flicked on a light. Maria knew the sun was setting and she needed to be home before her mother and Mr. Fox got back. "Let me ask Edward one more question."

Maria sat at the table and balanced the pen between her knuckles again. She was nervous with Sebastian standing beside her because she knew he was skeptical. She settled into stillness and waited. "Eddy?" she whispered. "Do you hear me? I'm ready." She shut her eyes and sat at the table and patiently waited for Edward to write through her.

But nothing happened.

She felt no cold tingle of air, no frost around her hand, no magic at all. She felt only the eyes of a nonbeliever and a caring Mrs. Fisher pressing into her. "Edward?" Maria began again, her voice shaking this time. "I need to know where the treasure is. Are you there?"

Still nothing.

The air around her remained the same temperature. Finally, Maria opened her eyes and said, "He's gone."

Sebastian shook his head. "It's not real."

Mrs. Fisher rested her hand on Maria's back and rubbed it gently. "There, there . . . We can find the treasure another time."

Maria pulled herself from her chair. "There won't be another time. I'm sorry, Mrs. Fisher. I've failed you."

"Oh, Maria," said the widow. She threw her arms around her. "You failed no one. Don't ever think that!"

Maria knew this might be her last visit with Mrs. Fisher. Soon she'd be on the road searching for another town where she could con widows and other lonely victims. She wanted to tell Mrs. Fisher everything, but it just didn't seem right. And besides, she needed to leave right then if she was to beat her mother home. She sniffled and pulled away. "I have to go. Goodbye, Mrs. Fisher."

"Goodbye, Maria," replied the widow. "And goodbye to you, Sebastian!" Mrs. Fisher stuck out her hand for a handshake. "It was nice to meet you! I do hope you'll both return soon."

Sebastian smiled and shook her hand. "It was a pleasure to meet you!"

"I'll prepare us all some lunch again," said Mrs. Fisher. "And I'll even have some of that favorite bread of yours, Maria."

Sebastian pulled on Maria's sleeve. "Why must we go so soon? If we call our parents, we can stay a little longer. It's not that I don't believe there COULD be ghosts. We just need to conduct some experiments to find out the truth."

Maria grabbed Sebastian's hand and tugged him through the door. "We're out of time. I'm supposed to be home now."

"But—"

"Let's go!" said Maria. She gave one last glance at the photos lining the walls and glared at the face of Edward seated in the crowd.

And then Maria realized something.

She hadn't let anyone down. It was Edward. He'd let them all down by disappearing again.

There probably was no hidden treasure to begin with. And why did she have to have Edward for a friend, anyway?

He couldn't hug her when things were awful.

And things were definitely awful.

He couldn't stop her mother from taking her away from her home. He couldn't cook her lasagna like Sebastian's mom. And he had a way of disappearing just when she needed him most. Right now would have been a good time to prove himself real to Sebastian!

She tore through the door with Sebastian trailing her and stomped down the old stairs. Sebastian argued as he followed behind her, but Maria paid no mind.

Nothing was going her way, and there was no way to fix things.

20
Friendship Derailed

The train rocked back and forth and echoed in the tunnel under the East River as it headed into Brooklyn. Passengers rested their heads in their hands or read newspapers. Two friends argued at the front of the train car. Sebastian held the pole and tried to balance while Maria positioned herself with her back against the door.

"W-w-what's going on?" Sebastian asked.

"Nothing. I mean . . . What do you mean?"

"First you make me pack up your apartment as if you're mov—" Sebastian's voice was swallowed by the screech of the brakes when the train pulled into High Street. "And there's nothing but junk food in your place! I packed candy and beef jerky."

"So?" asked Maria, gripping the pole as the train started again.

"Okay, well, what's with the prison quarters inside the closet?"

"What prison quarters?"

"Aw, come on! That little mattress and gray blanket under your mother's coats! Is that where you sleep?"

"Of course not!" Her eyes darted away from Sebastian's gaze. She couldn't look at him and lie. Telling him about Edward had been a big mistake. If Maria ratted her mother out by sharing her family's schemes, she knew she'd have to pay for it. She moved away, but Sebastian cornered her in front of a passenger with headphones.

"I've seen your whole apartment. There's nowhere else for you to sleep. That was your bed! And why did your mom force you to pack?"

"I told you! She's busy."

Sebastian shook his head. "And the ghost? How come you never told me about him?"

"It never came up."

"Do you talk to fairies too? Was there ever even a treasure?"

"I told you. It's just Edward, and he asked me to help Mrs. Fisher find her treasure. I've been relaying the clues to her so we can locate it."

"I don't believe anything you say. It all sounds made up!"

"I'm telling you the truth."

Sebastian slapped the door. "The truth! Your mother's

both a psychic and a social worker, but she hates visitors, and the only time you call me is when she's gone. But you're always scared she'll return. No one should be afraid of their mother!"

Maria couldn't handle Sebastian's questions, and there was nothing she could say that would pass for real with him. She'd seen how he lived. HIS life was normal. If she told him everything, he might tell his mother, and social services would be outside her door. They would take her away. What would her life be like, then? She had a good system living in the closet tucked away from everyone. There she could keep her secrets—like Edward—hidden.

The train pulled into Hoyt–Schermerhorn. Maria decided to change trains instead of continuing with Sebastian, but he hopped off with her.

"We had to leave Mrs. Fisher's place so soon. And what will your mother do if she gets home before you do? It's not even dinnertime."

Maria couldn't stand the idea of waiting on the platform for the G train, for who knew how long, with Sebastian pelting her with angry questions! He needed to shut up. She darted back onto the C train before the door closed.

The train stalled, and the doors opened again. Sebastian slid in through the partially opened door, his face raw and agitated.

"Don't squirm out of this like you always do! Like you did at the library with Ms. Madigan! You're always running away!" Sebastian was yelling at Maria. Passengers looked up from their reading.

"Mind your own business, Sebastian!" She pushed him in the chest, and he fell back. "Quit following me! You tag along asking me annoying questions. It's none of your business!" She pushed Sebastian again so that his back hit the door. "I LET you come over because you begged me. I LET you tag along to Mrs. Fisher's to find the treasure that YOU wanted to find. I didn't have to do that."

Sebastian raised his eyebrows before his eyes grew moist. Then he looked away.

"And furthermore, if I say to mind your own business, you need to do it! If you want to be my friend, you do as I say, or we're not friends!"

The train pulled away from Lafayette. There was only one more stop before she could get off.

"But I AM being your friend!" Sebastian said. "I'm trying to *help* you. Why did you run away from dinner at my house?"

Maria turned and faced the door that would be opening at her stop. The lights from the Clinton–Washington station grew brighter as the train approached.

Sebastian grabbed Maria's arm. "Just tell me what's going on so I can help! You're going to leave me, and you won't even talk about it. You just pretend like nothing is happening while all this weird stuff is tumbling around you!" Sebastian's voice cracked.

She had to protect herself.

The train screeched to a stop at the station, and the doors opened.

"Go away, Sebastian! We're no longer friends!" And with that, Maria tore herself away from his grip and fled down the platform.

21
A Missing Girl

ap! Rap! Rap!

Maria tossed and turned in the dark cavern of her bedroom.

Rap! Rap! Rap!

The heavy knocks shook the wall, waking Maria up. She opened one eye slowly.

It had to be her mother making that racket.

Maria pulled herself up from her mattress and stretched, glad to have the coats packed away so she could spread out.

"We got a customer!" said Madame Destine through the wall. The trot of heels echoed through the apartment until the front door slowly creaked open.

Maria wiped the sleep from her eyes and shook her head. Had she really gotten in a fight with Sebastian two weeks ago? She'd gone straight to her closet the night of their fight, beating her mother home by an hour. Maria had debated knocking on Sebastian's door, apologizing, and telling him everything. But something wouldn't let her do it, and with each passing day, the pain of not seeing him grew worse. A few clients had visited Madame Destine after seeing the flyers, which had kept her family from moving as they tried to gather funds for the road.

Maria placed one groggy eye against the hole that looked into the parlor. She could just make out her mom blocking the front door.

"I'm sorry to trouble you," said the voice at the door.

"Go on," said Madame Destine.

"I'm looking for a girl. She may have lived here. I'm hoping that I can find—"

"Step right in, my dear, step right into this parlor, and I'll *produce* the girl you speak of!" Madame Destine said with a bow. "For twenty dollars, I can supply *all* the answers!"

The lady hesitated before she walked in, her tiny figure and mass of curly hair backlit by the glow from outside. "I'm not sure I know what you mean," she told Madame Destine. The figure looked familiar to Maria, but she couldn't make out the details with her in silhouette.

"Come!" Madame Destine motioned for the lady to enter the parlor. "Have a seat! I, the great Madame Destine, will settle this matter for you!"

The tiny woman stepped into the parlor. Madame Destine pressed her hands on the woman's shoulders and drove her into the foldout chair. Once she was seated, the light from the window fell across the lady's face.

Maria gasped. It was Ms. Madigan!

But what was she doing in her house speaking to her mother? Surely she wasn't there to have a permission slip signed. Maria tried to swallow, but she couldn't. Then she broke into a sweat. There was nothing she could say or do behind the wall but watch with her eye glued to the hole.

"Now I need to visualize this lost girl," said Madame Destine.

"LOST GIRL! LOST GIRL!" echoed Houdini.

Madame Destine hit the cage hard. "Knock it off!" Feathers flew about the room, and Houdini went back to pecking at his seeds.

Maria's mother fanned herself to keep her composure. Then, in a gentler voice, she asked, "What's her age?"

"Shouldn't you know?" replied Ms. Madigan in a sharp tone. "I suspect she's ten or eleven. Brown eyes, curly hair. Skinny as a rail. Sweet as can be. You should know the age of your own—"

"SHHH! Don't tell me!" Madame Destine said. "I'm starting to visualize her!" Madame Destine's eyes opened wide, her irises becoming islands surrounded by white. "I need absolute silence!"

Ms. Madigan cleared her throat and began to tap impatiently.

Maria took a deep breath. She glanced around her room. Should she stay and continue this charade, or should she warn her mom? It was clear that she was the girl Ms. Madigan was looking for. Why her mother was unaware of this was beyond her. But then her mom had posted those flyers everywhere a couple of weeks ago.

Maria closed her eyes and waited for the familiar tingle against the back of her neck.

Nothing.

Maria sighed. Then she pressed her eye back against the hole and listened.

"Spirits of the next world. Tell me, *oh, tell me* where this girl may be!" Madame Destine said. "A young woman wishes to be reconnected with her!" Madame Destine shook and rattled her bracelets as she pretended to be possessed by a spirit.

This was not good. Not good at all, Maria thought.

"Honestly, Ms. Destine, I just need to know if she's here or if she's safe—"

Madame Destine grabbed Ms. Madigan's arm and pulled. "SHHHHHH!" she said. "She's here!"

Maria didn't know if she should turn on the fan. The loud clang of pipes beat through the apartment, and Mr. Fox's moans rang painfully in her ears. What was the point of continuing with this act? Ms. Madigan was not a gullible widow. She already suspected her mother of being involved with a fake nonprofit.

Ms. Madigan tapped her fingers on the table. "If she's here, I need to speak with her."

Houdini beat his wings in the cage.

Slowly, Madame Destine brought her head up from the table; her eyes rolled back in her head.

In a high-pitched voice, she said, "I'm here! It's so coooooold where I am now!"

Ms. Madigan lifted an eyebrow. "If this is some sick game, Ms. Destine, I'll have you know—"

"It's no game, Mommy. I'm here!"

Maria gritted her teeth. There was no way they would be staying in her apartment tonight. Within the hour, Ms. Madigan would send her family packing. Goodbye, Mrs. Fisher! Goodbye, Sebastian!

In a low and controlled voice, Ms. Madigan said, "I thought I'd seen it all until now!" She hopped off her chair and fumed. "I'm looking for *your* daughter, Ms. Destine! Is Maria here?"

Madame Destine's mouth fell open, and her eyes focused back on Ms. Madigan. "What?" she said.

"I'm here to find Maria Russo. I assume that you ARE her mother."

Madame Destine said nothing. She shook in silence.

"I've been calling your number, which was *supposed* to be a nonprofit, but after some research, I realized that, like this psychic act you're pulling, it's all a scam!"

Madame Destine looked worse than a teakettle about to steam. Her face was red and flustered. Sweat ran down her forehead; the black curls fell from her turban. Finally, she exploded, "Get out! Get out of my home!" She pushed Ms. Madigan so hard her back hit the wall.

The librarian stumbled. Then she straightened her posture and took deliberate steps to the door. In a shaky voice, she said, "I'll return for your daughter, Destine. But I'll be bringing Child Protection with me!"

Maria glanced at her mattress. The lump in her bed told her Sebastian was only a short distance away. She needed help, and she needed it now. Quickly, she dug under the bed for the walkie-talkie and turned up the volume. "Sebastian!" she called. "Are you there?"

"Get out of my hooooooome!" Maria's mother screamed through the wall. There was a loud crash. Then the pipes clanged and echoed loudly through the apartment as soft moans from Mr. Fox wailed from the kitchen.

"SEBASTIAN! ARE YOU THERE?" screamed Maria into the walkie-talkie.

Madame Destine's steps beat across the floorboards.

"Never in all my life have I seen such deception!" said Ms. Madigan.

"GET OUT OF MY HOME!" barked Madame Destine.

"Sebastian!" screamed Maria. "Answer me, please! I'm sorry!"

The clangs of the pipes died down, and the moans became soft whispers.

The front door slammed shut.

"OUT OF MY HOME!" echoed Houdini from his cage. "OUT OF MY HOME!"

Maria dropped her walkie-talkie on her bed and threw on her hoodie.

She burst through the door of her mother's closet and jumped onto the queen-size bed. The bedsprings grumbled as she crawled across it before she pulled the curtains away from the window. Then she used all her strength to pry open her mother's bedroom window.

"MAAAARIA!" shrieked her mother from the other room.

"MAAAARIA! MAAAARIA!" echoed Houdini.

Maria pulled half of herself out the window, the wind stinging her face and sending a chill through her. But her feet kicked back and forth inside the warm bedroom.

"Maria!!!!"

Maria pulled the rest of herself through the window. Then she jumped and caught hold of the bottom of the ladder of the rusty fire escape and pulled herself up.

"Maaaaaaaaria!" boomed her mother, her footsteps growing louder like an approaching thunderstorm.

Maria grabbed hold of the ladder and tried not to look down.

The fire escape swung a little in the wind, so she placed one foot ahead of the other and willed herself up the rungs.

The cool wind howled, drowning out her mother's screams inside. The fire escape clanged and moaned with her every step.

"Maria! Where are you?" screamed her mother from inside. "You double-crosser!"

"MARIA! MARIA!" echoed the parrot.

The noises grew faint as Maria reached the third story of the brownstone and beat on Sebastian's window.

"Sebastian!" she said. "I'm sorry about everything! I'll explain. Just let me in!"

The wind sent a shiver down Maria's spine. She stared at her blurry reflection in Sebastian's window. He was gone. Maria felt like she was trapped in a box of nails. However she looked at her situation, she was pricked with knowing she was helpless.

But then she saw him, and the pain stopped.

Sebastian held his walkie-talkie and spoke into it.

Maria rapped on the window. "Sebastian! Sebastian!"

He dropped the toy on the floor and rushed to the window. Then he unlocked the latch and pulled up the pane.

Maria scrambled to fit herself through the window. Arms in front, she pulled herself halfway through. Then she reached out for support.

Sebastian grabbed Maria's hands and pulled her the rest of the way in.

Maria shot through the window and tumbled to the floor.

"Sebastian!" she cried, trying to catch her breath. "I need your help!"

22
To Stay or Go

Maria told Sebastian everything.

She told him about her mother's scams, her tiny bedroom in her mother's closet, the phone calls her mother received from Ms. Madigan, and finally, what had just gone down.

Sebastian sat at the edge of his bed. He nodded every once in a while as Maria spoke, but said nothing. His fingers grabbed at the edge of his mattress, his knuckles turning a shade lighter.

When Maria had finished, Sebastian blinked only a few times, as if he was trying to process everything she'd told him.

Maria fell next to Sebastian on his bed. She felt relieved to have everything out in the open.

Sebastian reached for Maria's hand and took it in his. After some silence, he said, "We should tell somebody."

"Who?" Maria asked. "And what will happen to me if we do? Who'll take care of me?" Maria pulled her hand away from Sebastian's and studied his bedspread, rubbing her fingers over the soft fabric. She thought about the ugly gray one in her mother's closet and couldn't believe she'd been cooped up there her whole life. But she wasn't vindictive. "I don't want to send my mom to prison."

There had been times when her mother had been kind—before Maria's grandmother died and Mr. Fox started coming around. Madame Destine had been patient with Maria when she homeschooled her, teaching her to read. Maria knew there were perfectly ordinary parents who never read to their children. Her mother was not one of those parents. She'd told Maria she was smart and encouraged her to use her brain. There had been other times her mother had made Maria feel like she was important. Like when Maria designed the business card for the bait. Or when she had discovered that the fan could blow through the vent and make the wind chimes sing their sad spirit song. She couldn't turn her mother in.

"But, Maria! She's a criminal!"

"She's my mom!" Maria stood and shivered. The whole thing made her nervous. She tiptoed to the window and peeked over the ledge. The courtyard and roof of the shack where Mr. Fox worked were visible. "I don't want to double-cross her, but I don't want to leave town with her either."

"You should stay here with me," Sebastian said.

Maria shook her head. "I'm sure your parents don't want to adopt me. That's just *too* much to ask." And it really was. She liked Sebastian's family; they were nice. But could she ever make straight A's and win blue ribbons like he did? She wasn't sure if she could see herself as part of his family.

"Then you should call the police and tell them where you are," Sebastian said with authority.

Maria nodded. She figured an adult should know her whereabouts, and instantly she thought of Mrs. Fisher. She knew at that moment, Ms. Madigan was calling the police.

Then she scrunched her brow. Would she have to testify against her mom in court? She couldn't bear the thought. "I just wish Edward was here," Maria said. "He would tell me what to do. Even if it's always in riddles."

"Well, I think you should stay here," said Sebastian. "At least until my parents get home. If your mother comes knocking on my door, we won't answer until Mom or Dad gets here. They'll know what to do."

Maria glanced out the window.

Mr. Fox walked back and forth in the courtyard with boxes. "It looks like they're loading the van," Maria said. "Maybe they'll just go without me. It wouldn't surprise me if they did." Maria pressed her nose against the window.

Sebastian hopped off his bed, accidentally kicking his

walkie-talkie on the floor. "Well, I guess we won't be needing this anymore!" He bent down and scooped up the plastic toy and placed it on the bed.

Maria laughed. "Whoever thought a toy could come in so handy?" Then she pointed out the window. "Sebastian! Look!"

A familiar magenta turban hovered above a leopard-print coat and set off alarms in Maria's head. Standing below Sebastian's window, barking orders at Mr. Fox, was Madame Destine.

Maria backed away from the window and shuddered. "I can't look. What are they doing?"

Sebastian's glasses clinked the window. "It looks like all of the boxes are out of the apartment." He turned his hat around so that the bill was behind him, bringing him closer to the glass. "Mr. Fox is lounging on the boxes, and your mother is pointing to them.

Maria shut her eyes. "What else? Are they looking for me?"

Sebastian shook his head. "It doesn't look like it. Mr. Fox just kicked open the gate and now he's loading boxes into a van."

Maria swallowed. "And my mom?" she managed.

Sebastian furrowed his brow. "It looks like she's gone back inside for something."

Maria exhaled and approached the window again. "She probably went back for Houdini."

Sebastian took his nose off the window, leaving a smudge on the glass.

"I'm gonna call my dad and tell him to come home early." He pulled his cell phone from his pocket and pressed some numbers. After a few moments, Sebastian spoke into the phone. "Dad! Maria's in trouble. Please call me back when you get this!" Sebastian hung up and put the phone on his bed next to the walkie-talkie.

Maria glanced about Sebastian's room, taking in his dresser that was probably full of nice new clothes. She examined her patched-up jeans and her dirty T-shirt.

"Hey!" Sebastian said, his face back in position against the window. "I think they're leaving you!"

Maria peered outside the window and saw the gate slam behind Mr. Fox. She heard the heavy coughing of the van and then heard the engine rev. The wheels screeched, and the van peeled away from the curb.

They stood in front of the window for a long time.

Finally, Maria said, "Well, that settles it." She let out a long sigh. She imagined what would happen when Sebastian's parents came home for dinner. They would probably feed her and then call the police. Then she would have to make a report. She would be an orphan. And orphans had to be relocated to a foster family. Maria didn't like the idea of any of it.

But she would need to get her things.

Surely her mother had left *something* of hers behind.

After all, if Madame Destine had planned on skipping town without her, then she would have likely left her daughter's things behind. Like her library book.

Finally, Maria pulled herself from her thoughts and nudged Sebastian. "I need to get my stuff."

"You're going back down?"

"I might as well. I'll be right back up!"

"What if they return?"

"Why would they? What's left that they could possibly want?"

Sebastian picked up his phone. "Why don't you wait for my parents to get home?"

Maria thought about it for a second but didn't change her mind. "I won't be long."

"Okay. I'll be right here," Sebastian said. "If something happens, I'll call the police."

Maria nodded. She opened Sebastian's window and began to pull herself back through. Then she glanced behind her and gave a reassuring smile to her friend. She was glad she'd told Sebastian everything.

And she was happy to have him back in her life.

23
Danger! Danger!

Maria climbed through the open window in her mother's bedroom. She pulled herself across the queen-size bed, her face smashed against the mattress, until she was all the way through. Then she hopped off the bed and landed on the floor with a thud.

She scanned the room.

The bed was there, and so was the vanity dresser. But the boxes were gone.

She tiptoed into the kitchen, stepping on a Twinkie wrapper in the doorway.

The cabinets were all open.

She tiptoed back down the hallway and into the parlor. There was a light rectangle imprint on the floor where the rug once rested.

No cage. No foldout chairs.

Her feet echoed as she meandered down the long hallway from her mother's bedroom. As she walked, the temperature dropped.

"Edward?" whispered Maria. "Are you here?"

An icy chill whipped across her face. "What do you want?" she cried.

Maria rushed into the kitchen and scanned the table for the stack of paper. But there was none. She would have to get an explanation from Edward later.

The silence rang in her ears. She felt like she was inside a tomb, the remnants of what had once been her home. She rushed back into her mother's bedroom. Maria pulled on the handle of the closet as an icy chill stung her grip. "Ouch!" she cried. She grabbed the handle and yanked with all her might. The door flung wide open.

Strange.

Her mother's coats that had been packed away were hung back in their places. They were dark and heavy, dangling like bodies on a meat rack.

Maria's mattress was still there. All her things were exactly how she'd left them. She eyed the walkie-talkie on the bed and reached beside her mattress, gathering her few possessions: two white T-shirts, a faded pair of jeans, some gray underwear, and her library book.

The air chilled Maria to the bone. "Edward! Stop this," she pleaded.

She eyed a pen by the mattress.

Maybe it would be a good idea to find out what he wanted. "Okay," she said. "Tell me what I need to know!"

Maria rested the pen between her knuckles against the floorboards and waited. She could feel the icy air still slapping her face. "Edward! I'm ready! Just tell me!" she pleaded.

But Edward would not take her hand. Maria cleared her throat, closed her eyes and relaxed on her mattress. "I'm not going anywhere until you talk to me, Edward. You left me alone at Mrs. Fisher's when I needed to find her treasure. Don't leave me in the dark now!"

Finally, she felt the ghost's hand slide into hers. As she fell into her trance, the pen flung about in just a few squiggles before it dropped to the floor.

Maria opened her eyes and stared at the dusty wooden floor. She could barely make out the chicken scratch written on the splintered wood. Did it say *daNgEr*? Yes, it read *Danger!*

Maria read the word aloud: "Danger . . . Edward, I don't get it."

"DANGER! DANGER!" a voice echoed behind her.

Maria froze.

Where did that voice come from?

Ice slid down her back.

She took several shallow breaths, unable to control her breathing. Finally, she managed to get out a few words: "Who—Who—Who said that?"

But Maria would know that voice anywhere. She had

heard that voice in her dreams. It was the voice of obedience, the voice that echoed her mother's every thought.

Houdini.

If Houdini was there, then where was her mother?

Maria's eyes darted about the closet.

Next to her mattress were two worn pumps.

Tap.

Tap.

Tap.

One shoe rapped against the floor, patiently waiting for Maria to understand. Attached to it was a pale, thin leg, covered by a fake fur coat at the knee.

Angry eyes fell onto Maria, underneath a large turban.

"DANGER! DANGER!" cried Houdini, wobbling on Madame Destine's shoulder.

Maria's heart stopped.

All she could do was back against the wall and stare into the pale face that had been hidden with the coats.

Madame Destine doubled over with laughter while Houdini beat his wings about the closet. After catching her breath, she bellowed, "Maria! I knew you were talking to *someone*, but I had no idea that *someone* was Eddy!"

Maria froze.

How did her mother know Edward?

Had she even mentioned him in the closet? Yes, she had. She had asked him to tell her what was wrong. And then he wrote a message!

After Houdini settled onto Madame Destine's shoulder, she stroked his beak, before turning her gaze on Maria. "So this is what you do in here when I'm not looking," she said, motioning to the pen on the floor. Then Madame Destine kicked the pen out of the way as she stepped in front of the door to block Maria from escaping. "I heard your little toy buzzing in your room," she added, pointing to the mattress.

Maria swallowed hard.

She'd left the walkie-talkie on full volume before she fled.

"You *do* know you're forbidden to talk to other children."

Maria nodded, trying to swallow again. But she couldn't. Her throat was dry.

"Well, Maria, you're quite the little performer. You almost had me fooled."

The hairs stood up on Maria's arms as she remembered hearing Madame Destine say this when she'd answered the phone in her dream.

Where is he, child? Is he in here now?"

"Wh-wh-who?" Maria squeaked.

"Eddy. You in here, Eddy?"

"I don't know what you—"

"Save it, motormouth! I heard you say 'Edward'! I heard you say 'treasure.' I heard you say 'Mrs. Fisher'!"

Maria shook her head.

She was trapped. She pushed herself back and felt the hard plastic of the walkie-talkie dig into her back. She took

a deep breath. All she had to do was press the button and pray Sebastian was listening upstairs.

Madame Destine reached inside her coat and pulled out two white squares of paper. Slowly, she unfolded them. Then she read the first paper. "Tell her first: Remember the light of the silvery moon . . . and the honeymoon a-shining in June."

They were the messages Madame Destine had taken from under the fruit bowl. She had been holding on to them all this time!

Maria brought her hand behind her and felt the contours of the walkie-talkie until she found the button.

Then she pressed down on it.

Madame Destine brought the other message up to her eyes and cleared her throat:

"Poor, penniless Mrs. Fisher will miss the ring on her finger. But hidden inside her flat, her fortune rests untapped. Mr. Fisher hopes that you'll help her find what she will treasure."

"TREASURE! TREASURE!" echoed Houdini.

Madame Destine crumpled the messages and dropped them to the floor. "How long you been talking to Eddy? Tell me!"

Maria shook her head. "I don't know."

"Save it," said Madame Destine. Then she delivered a vile smile. "Well, this is all very surprising." She folded her arms and rested her weight against the door.

Madame Destine took up all the oxygen in the small, cramped space.

Beads of sweat formed at the top of Maria's scalp.

"You know, your grandmother had it. I always knew she could talk to them—ghosts." Madame Destine waved her hand in the air. "Me? Never could do it. But I guess Eddy's told you about me by now." Madame Destine reached down and stroked Maria's chin. "How long have you known?"

Maria tried to refrain from showing any emotion. One false move could set her mother off. But her heart was thundering inside. "Known what?" she gasped.

"That I'm not your real mother," she said, releasing Maria's chin.

Madame Destine wasn't her mother? But if she wasn't her mother, then where did Maria come from? "Who is my mother?" Maria managed to ask her.

Madame Destine shrugged. "Who knows! She died in a car wreck before I met your father." Then Madame Destine clapped her hands together. "But how wonderful it is you've known your father all this time!" She paused before curling her upper lip. "THAT DUMB POET DEADBEAT!"

Maria tried to think, but she couldn't. "Who?" she whispered.

"What was I supposed to do?" continued Madame Destine, ignoring Maria's question. "I was single, with two mouths to feed. Your grandmother loved you and offered to teach me the tricks of the trade if I took care of you."

Maria couldn't believe what she was hearing. Could that "dead-beat poet" be Edward? And Edward was her father? Madame Destine had told Maria her father had disappeared long ago. But he was a ghost.

No wonder he'd been talking to her all these years! He was trying to protect her. Protect her from Madame Destine. Her stepmother.

"My first thought was to get rid of you. I had to take care of myself. But when I looked into your eyes and held you in my arms, I knew I had to keep you as my own, so I gave you my last name." Madame Destine shut her eyes and smiled, cradling her arms as if she were holding a baby Maria. Then she stopped and opened her eyes. "Your father was never a stable man. You know what he left me after he jumped in the river?"

Maria shook her head, fighting back her tears. Her father must have taken his own life.

"Nothing!"

"NOTHING!" echoed Houdini.

"He left us not one thing to our name!" Tears swelled in Madame Destine's eyes. "I had only one choice if I wanted to feed you, Maria. There weren't many options for me then."

Maria found it hard to believe Madame Destine was playing the victim after lying to her about everything all these years.

"After your grandma died, someone knocked on my

door looking for her and I said, 'Sure. That's me.' And so I became *Madame Destine*."

Maria's finger was sore from pressing the button on the toy, but she didn't dare remove it. *Please!* she thought. *Sebastian, please be listening.*

"I had to do the only thing this family's known for! I had to talk to the dead! I had to *see* the future!"

Maria said nothing. This imposter had posed as a psychic and then as her mother.

"But it looks like we're in *luck*," continued Madame Destine. "Remember how I asked for one *teensy* last favor from you?" Madame Destine bent down so that her eyes stared straight into Maria's.

A favor? Maria wanted to run, but she didn't dare. She only shook her head slightly.

"We've got one last job to do before we skip town, and you're gonna bring me to it!"

Maria shook. "Wha-what is it?" she gasped.

"Take me to Mrs. Fisher's home and find me her treasure!"

Maria shook her head. "I won't do it."

"Oh, you'll do it, so help me!"

Maria shut her eyes. She wished this imposter would just go away.

"I'll take away everything you love. No pens. No library. No books."

Maria fought to hold back her tears.

"You'll take me to that treasure!"

Suddenly there was a knock on the door. Maria pulled her head up and wiped her eyes. Could it be the police? Could Sebastian have come to rescue her?

Madame Destine peeked behind the cracked door before she let it swing open. "I found her," she said under her breath. "She came back for her things."

Mr. Fox stood in the doorway like an undertaker waiting for a funeral.

He held a shovel in one hand and a sack in the other. "I buried the files and parked the van around back. Whaddya wanna do with the girl?"

"She's proven to be useful after all," replied Madame Destine. "We got one stop to make before we skip town. Did Mrs. Fisher leave her address with you after she made her donation?"

"That she did. It's in the log in the van."

"Let's go, then," said Madame Destine. "Get up, Maria. Move!"

Maria stood carefully, making sure she was pressing the button on the walkie-talkie. She followed her stepmother out of the closet, but just as she was about to turn into the kitchen—

CRACK!

The toy knocked out of her hand and hit the floor.

"You think you're so smart!" said Mr. Fox. "We won't be sending messages to our friends, will we?"

Maria exhaled before letting her shoulders sink. The walkie-talkie had been her only hope. Now it was smashed against the floor. She would never see Sebastian again. She hoped with all her heart that he had heard everything and would warn Mrs. Fisher.

"Let's go!" ordered Madame Destine. They left in a hurry.

As Maria stepped into the van, she looked one last time at her building, searching for Sebastian in his window.

24
Kidnapped

The sun melted behind the glass towers of the city, setting the city ablaze while the East River reflected the sky in fiery ripples. A white van hurtled through the flames, crossing the Manhattan Bridge.

Maria knelt in the dirty van, tucked between boxes. She tried to hold her balance, but the bumps jolted her this way and that.

Madame Destine and Mr. Fox bickered up front.

Maria blamed herself for this mess. Why didn't she listen to Edward's warning at home? And poor Mrs. Fisher! Nothing good would come to her after they arrived at her apartment. Now Maria was being taken away by a lady pretending to be her mother. She knew Madame Destine had conned every person who walked into their brownstone. But she'd never believed she'd been conned herself. Why hadn't Edward told her Destine was her stepmother? He'd told her she was smart and kind, but never who her parents were. He must have been trying to protect her from the truth. If Edward was her father, then who was her real mother?

Maria shivered, then rubbed her arms. "Oh, Edward?" she whispered. "Are you here?"

But the cold air did not answer back.

The van screeched to a stop, thrusting Maria forward. She wrapped her arms around her knees and shook.

All was silent.

Maria tried to collect herself. She had no idea where she was.

Two doors squeaked ajar at the front of the van. Then footsteps approached the back.

Screeeeech!

The van door slid open with one long swoop.

Mr. Fox and Madame Destine peered between the boxes at Maria curled in a ball.

"Get out!" Madame Destine ordered before slamming the front door.

"GET OUT! GET OUT!" echoed Houdini from her shoulder.

Maria took slow, deliberate steps away from the van.

Then Madame Destine and Mr. Fox each grabbed one of Maria's arms and pulled her forward, charging for the steps of Mrs. Fisher's apartment.

"Keep quiet and do as you're told," said Mr. Fox.

"Ring the buzzer!" demanded Madame Destine.

Maria shook her head. "I can't!"

"Oh, for crying out loud!" her stepmother fumed. She pressed the button long and hard. "Stay there and don't move!"

"DON'T MOVE!" echoed Houdini.

Maria couldn't stop from shaking. She heard the buzzer ring across the apartment. She searched Mrs. Fisher's windows.

They were dark.

Please don't be home, Maria thought.

But one light turned on. Maria caught her breath. Then she heard the familiar light steps of the widow descending the stairwell.

Madame Destine and Mr. Fox stood against the facade of the building on either side of the door.

Mrs. Fisher took a peek outside the small window at the entrance.

Maria frowned. She knew she was the only person in the widow's line of sight.

The door slowly creaked open. "Maria? Sweet child! What are you doing here after dar—"

"Good evening!" said Madame Destine as she pushed the door farther open. "Thank you for inviting us in!"

Her smile deflating, Mrs. Fisher glanced at Madame Destine and then at Mr. Fox.

The couple pushed Maria inside.

"I do believe you are acquainted with my daughter,"

said Madame Destine. "And you've also had the pleasure of meeting Mr. Fox." She slammed the door behind her and added, "We won't be long."

Mrs. Fisher brought her hand up to her heart, but Maria stared at her feet. Looking at Mrs. Fisher was just too painful. She'd led them to her.

Mr. Fox guided the widow up the stairs, and Destine followed.

Maria dragged behind, knowing each step brought her closer to Mrs. Fisher's apartment, away from anyone who could help them.

Once they reached the top, Mrs. Fisher let them in, and they filed in silence down the long hallway to the living room. Then Mrs. Fisher dropped to the edge of her sofa and placed her shaking hands in her lap. "I should have known Maria was yours the day she followed me home. What brings you here?" she asked, her voice quivering.

Maria tried to remain calm. She didn't want to be part of Madame Destine's pack. She wanted to be with kind people, like Mrs. Fisher. Maria fell beside the widow and buried her head in Mrs. Fisher's lap. "I'm so sorry," she sobbed. "I didn't mean to lead them here. Please don't hate me!"

Mrs. Fisher stroked Maria's head. Then she cleared her throat. "I don't know what plan you have going, but I have nothing of value here." Mrs. Fisher pointed her ringless finger at Mr. Fox. "That man took the last valuable thing I owned." Mrs. Fisher looked around her apartment, then shrugged. "But take whatever you want," she said. Then she lowered her head, and her voice softened. "Just leave Maria with me."

"Oh, give me a break," Madame Destine said, her upper lip twitching. "You *do* have something of value. I've received a message that there *is* a treasure here." Madame Destine checked her reflection in the full-length mirror and fluffed up her collar before she continued. "I tell you what. You provide us with the treasure, and I'll see to it that Maria isn't harmed."

Mrs. Fisher shook her head. "But there's no treasure. Not that I know of. Eddy never told us what it was."

Maria pulled herself from Mrs. Fisher's lap. "It's true . . . Edward never told us."

Madame Destine took a deep inhale but remained composed. "Then we will have to make Eddy tell us, won't we!"

Maria shut her eyes. "Edward?" she whispered. "Edward, if you're here, please tell us where the treasure's hidden."

The air did not stir around her.

Maria tried to hold herself together, but trembled. "He—he—he's not here."

Mr. Fox slapped the table. "What a load of bunk! How's this girl gonna find us anything?"

"Shhhh!" said Madame Destine. She took three steps before she stopped and erupted with laughter. "Oh, Eddy?

I know you're here. IF you truly love YOUR daughter, you WILL do as I say!" Her eyes darted about the room. "You'll tell us where the treasure is. And if you don't . . . Do you care about your daughter?"

Madame Destine yanked Maria by the hair so that she had no choice but to stand, leaving Mrs. Fisher behind on the sofa. "Have a seat at the table," said Madame Destine. "And get ready to write!"

Maria fell into a chair at the dining room table.

Mr. Fox found a blank sheet of paper and a pen and placed them in front of her.

Madame Destine rubbed her hands together while Houdini peered from her turban.

Mrs. Fisher quietly eased off the sofa and tiptoed to the hallway.

"Watch her!" said Madame Destine, and pointed at the widow.

Mr. Fox ushered Mrs. Fisher back to the sofa and stood beside her.

Maria shut her eyes and took a deep breath, trying to tune out Mr. Fox and Madame Destine.

"Edward?" she asked, and paused before her chin trembled. Then she blurted out, "I'm sorry. I did my best." Maria covered her mouth and shook before she regained composure.

But then she felt the slightest tingle.

Maria brought her head up and sniffled. "He's here."

She eased back in her chair and balanced the pen between her knuckles. An icy chill engulfed her hand, and before she knew it, she was in a trance. Her hand moved along the blank sheet of paper, this way and that, as fancy penmanship magically appeared where her hand traveled. Finally, the spirit left her. Maria's head fell back, the warmth returning to her.

Madame Destine snatched the paper from the table. "Finally! MY treasure!" she said.

Buzzzz! Buzzzzz! Buzzzzzz!

Lights flickered.

A gust of wind swept through the apartment and ruffled the curtains.

Archimedes hissed and hid under the sofa.

Slam!

Bam!

Ka-bam!

The doors in the apartment shut one by one.

Madame Destine's eyes were round and white as headlights, searching about the room for the cause of the disturbance. Slowly, she backed away from Maria, clutching the message. "E-E-Eddy? Is it you?"

Maria wondered the same thing.

Could Edward make doors slam? He'd never done that before. A tingle of excitement was all she could feel of his presence. At that moment, Maria wondered if her father had come to rescue her.

25
Cry of the Dead

"Desssssstine!" hissed a whisper in the hallway. "Dessstine!"

Madame Destine backed into the piano, her backside hitting some of the keys. She shot up and rubbed her arms. "Eddy?" she called. "Is it you?"

The light whisper continued. "Dessssstine! Let her go!"

Mr. Fox's jaw fell open.

Mrs. Fisher raised her hand to her heart.

Archimedes peeked from around the sofa again.

Houdini wobbled on Madame Destine's shoulder as her face lost all color.

But Maria was confused. If Edward could haunt like this, then why hadn't he done it before? Why did he write through her if he had a real voice? He'd never uttered a single word until now. His presence was always subtle, unnoticeable if she didn't know what to look for.

"Oh, Eddy! Are you coming for me?" cried Madame Destine. "I'm not ready!"

"Let . . . her . . . go!" the voice whispered.

Madame Destine dashed to Maria's chair. "Did you hear that?" she said. Madame Destine pulled the chair from under Maria so that she had to land on her feet. Maria rushed to Mrs. Fisher's side.

"I let her go!" said Madame Destine. "Eddy! D-d-don't hate me! I had my reasons. You *left* me, remember!" Madame Destine sank into Maria's chair. Her body seemed deflated, and her hair slipped from under her turban.

"I had no choice!" Madame Destine said. "I needed money! I had your daughter to care for!"

Mr. Fox scratched his head through his cap before raising a brow. He eased away from the living room and snuck down the long hallway toward the bedroom.

"I want you to go far away from this place," the voice whispered. "And never come back."

"Oh, Eddy! Please don't *haunt* me!" cried Madame Destine. "I'm sorry!" The fake psychic rolled her hands into fists and brought them to her eyes.

Maria squeezed Mrs. Fisher's hand and pointed. "Over there!"

A dark, cloaked spirit floated down the hall. The ghost seemed to drift lightly past Mr. Fox.

Madame Destine tore her hands away from her eyes before they widened. "Eddy! I had to do what I did to survive! You disappeared in the river! Remember?" Her body shook. She pushed her turban back in place and whined, "What do you want from me? What more can I do? Don't come for me, Eddy!"

The tiny banshee entered the living room in a mass of black—was it satin bedsheets? Maria took a shallow breath.

Mr. Fox tilted his head, scooting past the ghost before taking a deliberate step so that his shoe pinned down the tail of the floating bedsheet.

The ghost continued to float.

"Okay! You want me to change? Then I'll change!" screamed Madame Destine.

As the ghost moved forward, the sheet remained pinned under Mr. Fox's foot and gradually fell away.

Madame Destine's eyebrows arched. "You!" she said.

Then Maria saw him. It was Sebastian. The dark bedsheet lay limp on the floor behind him.

Sebastian stopped and looked around.

"Sebastian!" cried Maria. He *had* heard everything on the walkie-talkie. He *had* come for her!

Disgust overcame Madame Destine. "Sebastian?" she asked. "A dumb kid?" She darted her eyes around the room. "Well, Eddy. It looks like you're not coming for me, after all!" She pointed at Sebastian and ordered, "Tie him up with the widow!" Then she smiled, rubbing her hands together. "We've got a treasure to find, and Maria's gonna find it for us!"

Maria's eyes darted from Mrs. Fisher to Sebastian to Mr. Fox and finally Madame Destine. "But I haven't been able to decipher any of Edward's clues!" she said.

"You'll find me that treasure, Maria!" Madame Destine swung the message at her. "I'll give you five minutes to make sense of it. And if you don't, then say goodbye to your friends!"

Mr. Fox ripped the bedsheets into long strips and fastened them around the legs and wrists of Sebastian. He did the same to Mrs. Fisher.

Maria took the message. Then she held the paper up and tried to keep from shaking.

She couldn't swallow because her mouth was dry, but she knew her friends needed her.

Everything depended on her now.

26
To Solve a Riddle

Maria read the message:

You saw the perfect picture once,
In this very room.
The cat was cradled in your arms,
That sunny afternoon.

You have your kindred spirits here;
Those living just make two.
The treasure's hidden in the place
Reflected inside you.

Maria brought the message down to her side. Then she shook her head. How could Edward do this to her? He'd promised a real treasure for a widow with no money. Now he was telling her it was inside her.

"No," she whispered. "It's not that kind of treasure." She wiped her eyes before her face grew stern. "There's no gold and silver."

The floorboards creaked as Madame Destine snaked her way to Maria. Very slowly, she asked, "What do you mean?"

Maria lowered her voice and, without any emotion, replied, "There was never a treasure!" Then she mumbled, "At least, not your kind."

Maria watched her friends struggling to break free and felt pain. Then she turned to her stepmother.

"The treasure is about *love*," Maria said with certainty. Then she narrowed her eyes. "Somehow, I don't think it's what you were after."

Madame Destine crumpled the message and let it fall to the floor.

Houdini flapped his wings before he settled down again.

Madame Destine puffed up her fur collar. Then, in a soft voice, she continued. "If there's one thing I know about Eddy it's that his poems had multiple meanings. It's here. Find the treasure."

"FIND THE TREASURE!" echoed Houdini.

Maria shook her head. She wondered what Edward's real intention had been for her all along. Was she *supposed* to find something hidden in Mrs. Fisher's apartment? It seemed like he sent her on a treasure hunt in order to connect her with the widow. He must have waited all those years for Mrs. Fisher to come before he sent Maria after her. And now she'd been introduced to jazz, Beat poetry, and abstract art. That would explain why he never told her where the treasure was but kept sending her back so she could become acquainted with Mrs. Fisher and Sebastian. No. She knew now there was never an actual treasure.

Madame Destine placed her fingers lightly on the back of Maria's head, stroking it in soothing, gentle circles. "There must be something in this room that you saw," she cooed. "The poem stated, 'You saw the perfect picture once while standing in this room.'" Madame Destine gave a smile that was as red and ugly as a scab. Then she spun around and pointed to the wall. "Which painting is it? Which one is it hidden behind?" Maria's stepmother nudged Mr. Fox. "Turn over the paintings until you find a safe!"

Mr. Fox obeyed, ripping the artwork from the walls and knocking the African masks to the floor.

Mrs. Fisher flinched. "There's nothing in this room!" she said. "I've lived here for over sixty years! I think my husband would have *told* me if he had something of value hidden in here!" Mrs. Fisher struggled to break free again but gave up.

Maria knew it must have pained her to see her things so badly treated.

Sebastian tried to help the widow, but Mr. Fox had done a number on tying his knots.

Maria looked up. Maybe her stepmother was onto something. She was right about one thing: Edward liked to hide multiple meanings in one message.

She surveyed the room. There was the upright piano. At the far end of the room was the dining room table with all the books on top. The trunk where they had tea was just beside the sofa. Behind the sofa was a window and curtains. Then there was the hallway. The rest of the wall held more paintings and the full-length mirror.

Archimedes poked his head around the sofa. He dashed across the living room and down the hallway.

Maria shut her eyes.

She saw the picture of herself holding the cat. It was a bright afternoon, and everyone she loved was reflected behind her in the full-length mirror.

Slowly, she approached the mirror and studied her reflection. Mrs. Fisher and Sebastian were tied up on the sofa behind her. Mr. Fox was tearing down paintings. Madame Destine was rubbing Houdini's beak.

Could this be what Edward meant?

She pushed the full-length mirror.

Nothing happened.

She knocked on the glass.

It made a dull, hollow sound.

Maria scanned the room for something heavy. Then her eyes rested on a Grecian vase.

She hurried across the living room and stopped at the vase in the hallway. She bent over and used all of her strength to lift it. Then she gripped it and wobbled over to the mirror. Maria hefted the vase up to her shoulders. Then she hurled it at her reflection.

Crash!

Glass shattered. Tiny shards sprinkled in Maria's hair and about her feet.

Everyone froze.

When Maria had brushed away the tiny flecks of debris from her face, she found herself staring into a black hole. A light breeze blew through it. Where the mirror once stood was a dark passageway.

Mr. Fox dropped a painting and rubbed his hands.

Madame Destine's eyes grew large, and a smile crept across her face.

Clap.

Clap.

Clap.

She clapped her hands slowly and steadily as she made her way to the secret passage. "Well done, Maria. Well done."

"That goes down to the basement," said Mrs. Fisher. "My husband used it for business but sealed it up after his publishing company failed."

Madame Destine ducked her head inside the entrance and took one timid step inside the hole. Then she turned around and motioned at Mr. Fox. "Watch them!" She pointed at Maria. "You, follow me!"

"YOU, FOLLOW ME!" echoed Houdini.

Maria didn't know if she should obey or stay with her friends. She'd solved the riddle and found a secret entrance so her stepmother could retrieve the reward. But she knew better than to argue. It was Madame Destine calling the shots now.

She glanced back at Mrs. Fisher and Sebastian.

Mrs. Fisher nodded.

"Go," said Sebastian. "Just promise to come back."

Maria turned and took a deep breath. She brought one foot inside the hole and then pulled her other foot through.

Once Maria was inside the wall, Madame Destine grabbed her stepdaughter's hand. "You did good, Maria. I knew you were smart. Just like me."

Cautiously, Maria stepped into the dark. The musty scent of all things old filled her nose. She was overwhelmed with both dread and excitement.

Never had she dreamed she would get the chance to find a real hidden treasure. But part of her was also sad because she didn't want to find it this way. She wanted Mrs. Fisher to have it.

Maria wondered how long Madame Destine would hold her hand. Already her palm was beginning to sweat in her stepmother's callous grip.

But whether or not she was Maria's mother, Madame Destine had taken care of her since she was a baby.

Whatever the reason, it was clear that Madame Destine was not a good person.

One minute Madame Destine was tying up the people Maria loved, the next she was singing Maria's praises, depending on the circumstances.

Maria decided that whatever they found, Madame Destine could have it, but she would not be joining her in the getaway van. She loosened her grip and slowed her pace so that it was a strain to hold her stepmother's hand.

Maria let her fingers slip away from her stepmother's grip one finger at a time.

27
Buried with Treasure

Madame Destine stopped by a door at the end of the hallway and brushed away the cobwebs from the knob. She turned the handle, and the entrance creaked open.

Maria took in the strange scent. It smelled like old paper.

Madame Destine rubbed her hand against the wall inside until she found a switch.

The lights flickered on to reveal a wooden stairwell.

"Go first!" whispered Madame Destine. "We'll let your *father* protect you!"

Maria squeezed past Madame Destine and descended the crooked wooden steps. The lights only reached the first three stairs.

Then there was darkness.

One by one, Maria descended the stairs. Each step

moaned as she made her way down. "Edward?" Maria whispered. "Are you here?" This must have been the secret room where people drank alcohol and hid from the law! It must be the same room used to hide the treasure.

She wished she had a candle or a flashlight. No wonder her stepmother wanted her to go first.

Maria wondered, if something happened to her, would Madame Destine leave her there? She held on to the wall for balance while she descended, until her foot reached the tile of the floor.

Maria's eyes adjusted to the darkness. The distant lights above gave only hints to the contours of objects within the room.

There were large rectangular slabs set in circular rows that resembled the pictures of Stonehenge she'd seen in books. *Maybe this was an ancient place of worship,* Maria thought.

She felt Edward's presence against the back of her neck. "Edward?" she called. "What is this place?" But she knew he wouldn't answer back.

Maria swung her hands around until she felt a string hanging. She gave it a hard yank.

The lights buzzed momentarily before they lit across the room.

Maria smiled.

The monoliths were not pillars of stone. They were shelves. Row after row of shelves, holding hundreds of books.

Madame Destine's footsteps crashed down the steps behind her. Once her stepmother had a chance to glance about the room, she grew impatient. "This is the treasure?" she cried. "Books?" Where's the gold?"

"GOLD! GOLD!" echoed Houdini, perched on Destine's shoulder.

So, the treasure is a library, Maria thought. She took in the room. Strange abstract paintings hung along the walls next to boxes of what appeared to be more books. Maria tilted her head to read the titles on the spines. A lot of them seemed to be the same volume.

She picked one up. It was just a book of poems. On every other page were prints and small works of art.

Madame Destine swung her arms, knocking books from the shelves. "I don't believe it!" She spun around and called, "John! John! Then she stomped up the stairs, leaving Maria alone to explore.

The room was wonderful!

The paintings were dabs of thick paint applied in abstract fields of color on the canvases—like the ones she'd seen at the Museum of Modern Art. And the books! She strummed her fingers against the volumes lining the shelves.

Then Maria saw something—a book pressed farther off the shelf than the others. She dashed across the tiles and stopped in front of it. She reached out and pulled it from the row. It was thin, with a dusty green cover. The front read "*Ghosts and Other Poems* by Edward De la Cruz." Eddy De la Cruz was her father. Could this be his book?

Maria felt her throat close up. She fell to her knees, opened the cover, and buried her nose in the pages. They were poems—much like the ones he had written her all these years. Yes—it was her father's book! A sealed envelope fell out from the pages. Maria wiped her eyes.

The stairs grumbled as Madame Destine led Mrs. Fisher, Sebastian, and Mr. Fox down into the library.

"I'm allergic to dust mites," Sebastian protested between sneezes.

"Shut your trap!" snapped Mr. Fox. He pushed Sebastian forward so he bumped into Mrs. Fisher and Mrs. Fisher bumped into Madame Destine. The two hopped down the steps until they reached the floor.

Then Mrs. Fisher bubbled with delight. "The treasure is books! Oh, Robert!" She waddled up to the shelves, pressing her face to the spines. "These are my husband's books, the ones he published!" Mrs. Fisher chuckled, then looked around her. "And the paintings!" she added. "Robert told me he sold them! I guess he couldn't bring himself to do it!"

So this is what it's all about, Maria thought. Edward had wanted to connect them to Mr. Fisher's books.

But something didn't add up.

"Why did Mr. Fisher want you to find this library *now*?" Maria asked Mrs. Fisher.

The wrinkles in Mrs. Fisher's forehead lifted. "These

writers were my friends! Robert published them up until he quit, a year before his death!" A smile stretched across Mrs. Fisher's face. "I'm surrounded by the spirits of everyone I loved!"

It suddenly occurred to Maria that some of these were the missing works the librarian from the Berg Collection had hinted at—the Beat poets. But how much could they be worth?

"Maria," began Sebastian, "it's the—"

Maria gave Sebastian a quick nod and motioned with her finger to zip his lips.

"What's that?" said Madame Destine.

Sebastian looked down.

Mr. Fox dropped a stack of books, and they hit the floor with a loud bang. "What a load of bunk!" he snarled. "Where's the loot?"

Madame Destine paced back and forth, shaking her head. "There ain't any loot, you fool!" She pointed to Sebastian and Mrs. Fisher. "We got witnesses, John! How should we handle them?"

Mr. Fox's Adam's apple moved up and down as he swallowed. After a long pause, he said, "We'll leave them here and lock the door. Then we boogie out of town."

"You can't lock us down here!" said Sebastian. He lunged for Mr. Fox but stumbled over a box. "People will be looking for us!" he said, out of breath.

"Precisely," said Madame Destine, stepping over him.

"We'll leave the two of you here to rot with these books!" Madame Destine pushed up her turban. "And if you get bored, you can always *read*!"

Madame Destine rubbed her parrot's beak. Then she said, "See you in another life!" and took a bow. She grabbed Maria's arm and motioned for Mr. Fox to follow.

Maria pulled away. "I'm not going!" she exclaimed.

"What?" said Madame Destine. "Of course you are! I've got big plans for you, Maria!"

"What do you mean?" Maria said, glancing at her friends by the books.

"I'm going to make you famous. People will come from miles around to hear you talk to the dead. You'll predict the future, and I'll be your manager."

Maria frowned. "I won't do it."

"You'll do as I say."

Maria shook her head. "No, I won't."

Mr. Fox placed two calloused hands on Maria's shoulders. "Don't talk back to your mother," he snarled.

"I said no! And she's not my mother!"

"But think of all the people you can help." Madame Destine began with a plea. "You've always cared about doing the right thing. This is right! Don't you see?"

Maria paused to consider life in the limelight. Did people coming from miles around need to be told what the future would hold for them? Did they need to dig up the past to talk to the dead? Or was it better to live in the present? She didn't want to be responsible for the outcomes of people's futures. She wanted her friends. She wanted a family. And Madame Destine didn't know a thing about either.

"Leave me here," Maria said. "I don't belong with you."

Mr. Fox and Madame Destine gave each other a knowing look and locked arms around Maria. Then they dragged her up the stairs kicking and screaming. Maria put up a fight, but she wasn't strong enough to tear away.

"Let me stay!" cried Maria. "Leave me here! Let me stay!"

Madame Destine ignored her, stopping at the top of the stairs and looking below. "Good night!" she said, and slammed the door, muffling the cries of Mrs. Fisher and Sebastian.

Mr. Fox and Madame Destine pulled Maria through the secret passage, over the broken glass, and into Mrs. Fisher's living room. Then Mr. Fox pushed the piano in front of the hole in the wall, wiping the sweat from his brow when he was done.

Maria lowered her head and gave up her struggle. She couldn't overcome both her stepmother and Mr. Fox.

28
Houdini's Magic

adame Destine cracked the front door of Mrs. Fisher's building and poked her head out. She looked left and then right. Then she turned around and motioned with her eyes to Mr. Fox. With locked arms around Maria, they shot for the white van. Mr. Fox fumbled with his keys until he found the right one.

Madame Destine's nails dug into Maria's upper arm, but Maria didn't feel it. She was numb now and retreating far inside herself, into a tight space protected from the reach of anyone. She felt as if her heart was a water balloon that had been dropped from the top of a building. Now she was flat, a shattered remnant of who she once was—a mess on the cold sidewalk.

Heavy steps hammered the pavement behind Maria. She twisted her neck to see what it was.

A man was approaching them. He wore a black uniform and had a familiar wave of gray hair that swooped high above his forehead, resting over his ears.

It was Officer O'Malley!

He stopped beside them and placed his hand on Madame Destine's shoulder. "Excuse me, are you Destine Russo?"

Madame Destine's eyebrow leapt into her turban. She opened her mouth and nodded yes but said nothing. Her parrot moved down her arm, flapping his wings.

Officer O'Malley turned his gaze on Maria, and his face softened. "And is this your daughter, Maria?"

Madame Destine backed into the van. Then she quickly nodded.

The officer pulled out his wallet and allowed it to drop open, revealing his police badge. "I'm Officer O'Malley," he said. "I have a few questions."

Maria pulled her arm away from her stepmother and took tiny steps backward until she stood beside Officer O'Malley.

Mr. Fox was frozen with the van door half-open.

Car doors opened up and down the block as police officers stepped out from their vehicles.

Then sirens grew louder and louder into a deafening, maddening blaze of noise. Two police cars sped up to the curb and screeched to a halt. Doors flung wide open.

The toothpick figure of Ms. Madigan hopped out

from an open door. Her heels clicked against the sidewalk quickly. Two officers followed closely behind her.

One of them grabbed Mr. Fox and carefully shut the door to the van.

The other police car spit out Mr. and Mrs. Goldstein. "Sebastian?" called his mother, but the officers detained Sebastian's parents away from the van. "Maria! Where is Sebastian?" she called.

Maria began to breathe again. Helpers had arrived!

Officer O'Malley continued. "We've received two calls about a girl named Maria Russo." He patted Maria on the head. "One was from a librarian named Ms. Roxy Madigan. The other was from a child named Sebastian Goldstein." He took a step toward Madame Destine. "May we have a word with you?"

Madame Destine was frozen for a few seconds; her eyes darted from cop to cop as if she was weighing the odds of escaping. A female police officer grabbed Houdini from her arm and cradled the bird in her hands. Madame Destine protested but quickly gave up. Then she cleared her throat and meekly responded, "Sure, Officer. Have I done something *wrong*?"

Ms. Madigan pointed to Maria a couple of yards away. "That's her! That's the girl! Thank god she's okay!" But the officers held the librarian away.

Maria took a deep breath as she began to process what was happening around her. Was she going to be okay?

Madame Destine's voice shook. "I think there's been some kind of mistake, Officer. We were just on a family outing. Is there anything wrong with that?"

"We've received reports about the abuse of a Maria Russo and a missing child report for a Sebastian Goldstein from his parents. This same *Sebastian* called in a report two hours ago about a girl with the same name. He said she could be found at this address." He paused and looked at Maria. "And so we've found her."

O'Malley faced a thin officer with a bushy mustache. "Check the van for a missing boy." He turned around, placing his hand on Madame Destine's shoulder. "We would like to bring you down to the station for questions." Then he motioned to Mr. Fox. "You too."

Madame Destine fluffed her coat. "The trouble IS, Officer, we need to get my daughter some help. I would be happy to answer questions after we take her to the doctor. You see, she's not well."

Detective O'Malley cocked his head. "I'm not sure I'm following you."

Madame Destine spoke with confidence. "Well, for starters, she's been acting strangely. She's been missing from home for extended hours against my wishes. Now she tells me she talks to *ghosts*. I have no doubt there have been strange re—"

"It's not true!" screamed Maria. Madame Destine was twisting things, and it made Maria's blood boil. Who cared if Destine took care of her and fed her when she was young? The woman was a crook, and she had to be stopped before she hurt more people.

O'Malley gave Maria a curious look. Maria couldn't believe she had blurted it out. But she had to take a stand. If there was any justice in the world, surely the policeman could see she was good and Madame Destine was not.

Officer O'Malley looked with sympathy at Maria. Maria glared back at her stepmother. "There's nothing wrong with me!"

Madame Destine pointed to Ms. Madigan. "And yes, *that* lady has been by my home. No telling what my daughter told her, but I assure you that no law has been broken."

Officer O'Malley pursed his lips.

"Oh dear, Officer!" bellowed Madame Destine. "If ONLY I could control my daughter!" She brought her hand up to her turban and feigned fatigue.

"Liar!" said Maria. "I'm not causing trouble!" It felt good for Maria to finally say it! "I was only trying to find Mrs. Fisher's treasure!"

"Ha!" Madame Destine slapped her knee. "*Treasure?* Officer, my daughter gets these ideas in her head, and they're not *right*." Madame Destine tilted her head, her eyes watery and her voice trembling. "I just want to get her *help*."

"Liar!" said Maria. "She's twisting things again!"

"Don't call your mother a liar!" said Mr. Fox. "I can vouch for Destine. Her daughter's a troublemaker!"

Officer O'Malley scrunched his brow while bringing his hand through his wavy hair. He appeared to be thinking, pressing his lips together while the lines on his face grew heavy.

"You have to believe me," Maria said. "You need to rescue my friends."

Then the female police officer tapped him on his shoulder. "I think you need to hear this."

O'Malley stepped away from the van to a crowd of cops surrounding Houdini. The parrot rested on the hood of a car and seemed to be entertaining them.

"FORTUNE!" screeched the parrot. "DO TIME! GETAWAY VAN!"

An officer patted the bird's head. "Tell us more!"

"LAST CON! FIND THE TREASURE!" Houdini shouted. "TIE-EM-UP! TIE-EM-UP!"

"Shut up, bird!" said Madame Destine.

"OPPORTUNITY!" called the parrot.

"Knock it off!" said Madame Destine.

"KNOCK IT OFF!" echoed Houdini, sounding just like Madame Destine.

Officer O'Malley took three long steps back to the van until he stood directly in front of Maria. Then he bent down with his hands on his knees so that he was eye to eye with her. He asked in a sympathetic tone, "A treasure? And Mrs. Fisher?"

Maria pointed to the building behind her. "My stepmother

and Mr. Fox tied her up with Sebastian inside her apartment. We've got to help them!"

Officer O'Malley eased back up to his full height. He glanced at Madame Destine and Mr. Fox. Then he turned to an officer. "Take them in," he ordered.

The policewoman slapped handcuffs on Madame Destine and Mr. Fox while she read them their Miranda warning. Then she escorted the pair past Mr. and Mrs. Goldstein and Ms. Madigan before stuffing them into the police car.

"You won't get rid of me, Maria," screamed Madame Destine, blocking the entrance to the car. "You think you're clever, but I MADE you that way." The officers pushed her head into the car, but she fought back. "You can't stomp me out!"

Detective O'Malley gently placed his hand on Maria's back. "Can you take me to Sebastian and Mrs. Fisher?"

Maria felt like herself again. Her heart was a balloon filled with helium, and her spirit had lifted all the way to Mrs. Fisher's windows. Then a smile lit across her face. "Yes," she answered. "Follow me!"

29
The Ghost of a Family

The police marched in and out of Mrs. Fisher's apartment, her doors propped permanently open to keep the flow of them moving through.

An officer carried a cup of coffee and a paper bag of doughnuts past the piano, where a policeman was sweeping up glass. He ducked through the hole in the wall and charged down the long hallway, around the door, and down the rickety old stairs to the library. He entered the circle of library shelves where Officer O'Malley was talking to two kids and an elderly woman. He placed the bag of doughnuts on the stack of books and gave the cup of coffee to Officer O'Malley, who nodded before taking a sip.

"Now, where were we?" he asked.

Mrs. Fisher's hands rested on Maria's shoulders. Sebastian stood in front of his parents next to Maria.

Officer O'Malley's notepad was filled with three stories,

all intersecting and adding up to one incredible truth. He stroked his chin. "We'll have to get Destine's story and John Fox's, but it looks like we have enough evidence here to open up several investigations against them."

Maria glanced at Mrs. Fisher for some reassurance.

Mrs. Fisher forced a smile.

"Now, Maria," Officer O'Malley said with some hesitation. "We'll need to set you up with Child Protective Services and find a place for you to stay until everything is situated."

Maria slumped her shoulders. She had faced so many of her fears today, but she'd forgotten to consider what would happen if she turned Madame Destine in.

Of course she needed foster care. Someone had to take care of her.

Maria squeezed Mrs. Fisher's hand. "Can I stay with you?" she asked.

Mrs. Fisher gave Maria a sympathetic look. "Oh, sweetie, I would love that. But I don't know if I can afford to take care of you."

Maria's hopes plummeted. But then she remembered something. What about the books? She looked at Sebastian. "How do we know for sure if those books are worth more than gold?"

Sebastian nodded. "Well, remember that a first edition of *Ulysses* was worth close to forty thousand dollars! These books would have to be worth something. No one's seen them!" The two kids turned around and saw Ms. Madigan talking with a policeman.

"Let's ask Ms. Madigan what she thinks!" said Sebastian.

"Ms. Madigan, can you take a look at these books in the library and tell us what they're worth?"

Ms. Madigan stopped her conversation with the officer. "You want me to appraise these books?" she asked, a little confused.

"Just take a look," said Sebastian. "It may be the treasure we're looking for."

Ms. Madigan went down to the secret room and thumbed through the books in the late Robert Fisher's library. After she studied them and checked the publisher and date of publication on a few of them, her face lit up. "Actually, I think you kids are right!"

The three of them rushed to Mrs. Fisher, who was still talking with the detective.

"Mrs. Fisher? I'm Roxy Madigan, and I hope you don't mind me looking through your books!"

"It's not a problem!" said Mrs. Fisher. "I can't say the books are on the top of my mind right now."

"This may not be the time and place to talk about it, but *these* books are rare," said Ms. Madigan.

"It's true!" said Maria. "This really is the treasure that Edward sent me after."

"I know," Mrs. Fisher said. "Some of them have never seen the light of day. Poor Robert closed his press before—"

"Yes!" interrupted Ms. Madigan. "But a lot of these books are worth some serious money. There are collectors that would pay a hefty price for some of these never-before-seen works."

"I bet that man at the New York Public Library would like to get his hands on these," added Sebastian.

Mrs. Fisher patted down a tuft of hair. "Do you think so?"

"Of course!" the three of them said in unison.

"They're not only rare," said Ms. Madigan, "but a lot of these works couple Beat poets with prominent artists of the day. These works of art are extremely collectable."

Maria smiled. This *was* the treasure worth gold and silver! Mrs. Fisher would no longer be poor! And if Mrs. Fisher wasn't poor, then maybe she could be her caretaker!

"By the way, thank you for all that you've done for this child," responded Mrs. Fisher. She squeezed Maria's hand.

"I took a risk visiting your home, which is against policy," Ms. Madigan said, nudging Maria. "But I've been watching you for some time. I knew SOMETHING wasn't right. You're going to be safe now, Maria."

"Thanks for all your help." Maria said.

"And I'm going to research where you can take these books. There are collectors, yes, but you may even look into reprinting some of these works with larger publishing houses."

Then Maria remembered. There *was* a valuable book in that room!

She tore away from Mrs. Fisher and Ms. Madigan and slid across the tile floor until she found the place where she had dropped it. Her father's book had not been bothered in all the commotion.

She turned to the back flap where a picture of a middle-aged Eddy De la Cruz stood next to a beautiful woman and infant. Under it was his bio:

Eddy De la Cruz grew up in Puerto Rico but has called Brooklyn his home since 1975. He met his wife, Oriana, who came from a long line of psychic mediums, at a séance. When he's not writing poetry, he spends his spare time playing jazz records, practicing meditation, and caring for his child, Maria.

Maria stared at the photo of her family and studied her mother. She shared her same curly hair and large brown eyes, just like her grandmother. She shut the book and held it close to her chest. Somehow, she knew that things were going to turn out okay.

"Dad," she said, "thank you!"

Next to her was the envelope that had fallen out from the book earlier. Maria turned it over to discover that it was addressed to Mrs. Fisher.

Maria hopped up and rushed to the widow, handing her the letter. "Mrs. Fisher, this is addressed to you! Read it."

Mrs. Fisher carefully opened the envelope and took out

a yellowed sheet of paper with a handwritten note. "My dearest Marilyn," she read, her voice trembling with excitement, "I couldn't bring myself to sell off the book collection after I closed the press. My hope is that the books and paintings will increase in value long after I'm dead. Once you find this, take the collection and sell it at Sotheby's. Then use the money to do what you love. Forever yours, Robert."

Mrs. Fisher shut her eyes, placing her hand over her heart. "Robert," she said, "I know just what I'll do. Thank you!"

30
Joining the Living

Birds chirped outside. Traffic swooshed by like the ocean tide. Houdini perched in his cage by the window and pecked at some seeds in his bowl. "KNOCK IT OFF!" he shrieked.

Archimedes sat just under the bird, his green eyes watching the parrot's every move. The sun poured through the window and spilled onto the living room floor, the light broken only by the soft current of rolling shadows caused by the curtains. Piano keys rolled between the light voice of Mrs. Fisher as she played. "To our honeymoon, honeymoon, honeymoon a-shining in June!" she sang.

Suddenly a whistle blew in the other room.

"Tea's ready," said Mrs. Fisher before she shot up from the bench and scurried down the hallway.

Maria blew the hair out of her eyes and watched the shadows swim across her paper. Next to her was her own loot from Mrs. Fisher's treasure: her father's book of poems. She crouched on the living room floor surrounded by clumps of crumpled paper. Flat sheets of blank paper lay directly in front of her. She held the pencil—not between her knuckles, but the way a writer would. Maria's handwriting dipped and sank across the page, struggling to stay afloat. Scribble after scribble, she'd searched for the right words, but they hadn't surfaced.

It had all been so easy for Maria to write when Edward was guiding her hand, but it had been months since she'd felt his presence. Here she was. Writing the hard way. She wrote down the letters for her father, and those letters formed words addressed to anyone who cared, and those words made sentences that had been labored over for the love of every lonely soul—every girl who had read in secret in a tiny walk-in closet.

Only she was no good at any of it.

She sighed and wished she could connect to her father again. But if Maria was going to write, she was going to have to work at it. And the work was not easy.

The squeaky wheels of a cart turned into the living room.

Archimedes diverted his attention from Houdini only for a second.

"How's your work coming along?" Mrs. Fisher asked. "Are you having any luck channeling your father?"

Maria shook her head. "The words don't flow so freely anymore," she whined.

"It took the Beats YEARS of practice to channel their subconscious." Mrs. Fisher stopped the cart by the trunk. Then she smiled and poured a cup of tea. "And, sweetie, you're only eleven years old! You've got your whole life ahead of you to write poetry!"

Maria took the cup of tea from Mrs. Fisher and collapsed into the cushions on the sofa.

After the police had caught Madame Destine and Mr. Fox last October, Maria had been placed in a foster home by Child Protective Services, but Mrs. Fisher kept her promise and visited her regularly. Maria was aware that there had been a speedy trial, but she didn't have to testify at any of the hearings.

In between the court dates, Mrs. Fisher and Ms. Madigan catalogued the books and sold many to collectors willing to pay a high price. The paintings were auctioned at Sotheby's, and the bids were generous. By May, Mrs. Fisher's finances were in order and she was able to sign the paperwork to be Maria's legal guardian.

Maria took in the surroundings of her home.

The upright piano rested by the tribal masks, hung in their proper places. The full-length mirror had been replaced—only it had been reinstalled as a revolving door. She and Mrs. Fisher had agreed that they should keep the secret passage.

Maria leaned back on the sofa and took a gulp of tea.

BUZZZZZZZZZ BUZZZZZZ! BUZZZZZZZZZZ BUZZZZZZ!

"Good heavens!" exclaimed Mrs. Fisher. "Are we expecting anyone?"

Maria leapt over the sofa, landing by the window. Then she leaned out so her feet were barely touching the floor.

The warm sun felt good against her face. She peered over the ledge and saw the familiar red baseball cap of Sebastian below. "Who goes there?" she called in her pirate's voice.

Sebastian glanced up at her and smiled his gap-toothed grin. "I'm looking for buried treasure!" he yelled back.

Maria smiled. "Arrrrr, matey! I'll be right down!" She ducked her head back through the window and darted across the living room and down the hallway. "I gotta go!" Maria called from the door, almost out of breath. She reached for the handle before she added, "Sebastian's here!"

"Off!" Mrs. Fisher said, motioning with her hands for Maria to leave. She chuckled to herself and added, "Join the world of the living!"

Maria glanced back and smiled at Mrs. Fisher. *Buried treasure, indeed,* she thought. *What could be more priceless than friends?* Then she raced down the stairs, opened the front door, and stepped out into the warm spring day.

Author's Note

Although the story and characters in this novel are fiction, many of the references to art from Mrs. Fisher's past come from real life. In fact, Mrs. Fisher was inspired by the real-life jazz singer and pianist extraordinaire, Blossom Dearie, who performed in Greenwich Village well into her late seventies.

Nineteenth-Century Spiritualists and the Birth of Modern Art

Spiritualism is a religion that began in 1848; its practitioners communicate with ghosts through a medium, also known as a psychic. The spiritualist mediums talk to ghosts in a variety of ways, one of them being through *automatic writing*. This occurs after the medium meditates and *spontaneously* writes a message without thinking ahead what she would like to say, believing that a spirit is guiding her hand. Many writers say that automatic writing comes from the subconscious, an idea also utilized by early modern art movements such as the Surrealists (who wrote from a dream state) and the Beats (who wrote from a meditative *flow state*).

1950s New York and Greenwich Village

After World War II, the cultural focus shifted from Europe to the United States, and New York City became a vibrant place for artists to live. Moving into *cold-water flats* (apartments that didn't even have hot water) in run-down neighborhoods of lower Manhattan such as Greenwich Village, artists could share ideas in neighborhood clubs and cafes while surviving on very little money. Clubs like the Village Vanguard and Café Wha? popped up in the neighborhood, too. They showcased stand-up comics like Lenny Bruce, and jazz musicians such as Dizzy Gillespie, Miles Davis, and Charlie Parker. Artists took over lofts that allowed for plenty of light to paint, and writers penned their manuscripts in late-night cafes. Miles Davis came out with his album *Birth of the Cool*, and a group of writers became known as the Beats. It wasn't long before the term *beatnik* described the 1950s hipster: someone who lived on strong coffee and jazz, loved modern art and Beat poets, and lived in Greenwich Village.

The Beats

The Beat poets were an informal group of writers whose core members, Jack Kerouac and Allen Ginsberg, met while attending Columbia University in 1944. The group of writers expanded to include Neal Cassady and William S. Burroughs, among others, and they held informal meetings in Times Square diners to discuss their ideas. They would later travel across the country and set up shop in San Francisco. Jack Kerouac was the most popular of the writers, typing *On the Road* (1957) on a continuous scroll of paper so as not to interrupt his flow. Allen Ginsberg's poem "Howl" (1956) was controversial, giving the Beats notoriety with mainstream society by rejecting materialism and embracing Eastern spirituality. By the late 1950s, the Beats had brought counterculture to the masses and were the forerunners of the hippie movement of the 1960s.

The New York School of Abstract Expressionist Painters

While the Beats were developing their own style of writing, the abstract expressionist group of painters in New York City were inventing an American style of art that would differ from what was happening in Europe. Painters like Jackson Pollock, Franz Kline, and Willem de Kooning flung, dripped, and glopped paint onto canvas, calling their method *action painting*. It emphasized the physical process of painting instead of depicting actual subject matter. Peggy

Guggenheim, whose uncle Solomon Guggenheim founded the Guggenheim Museum, championed these artists, bringing them into the spotlight and helping to establish New York as the destination for modern art.

Jazz Improvisation

When musicians improvise, they invent melodies on the spot without knowing what they will play beforehand. Sometimes it comes together in harmony, while other times it can be discordant. Jazz musicians like Dizzy Gillespie and Charlie Parker developed improv into a new staccato, wild sound called bebop in the mid 1940s, playing in small clubs in Manhattan. By the late 1950s, they had influenced Thelonious Monk, Charles Mingus, Miles Davis, and John Coltrane, and long, melodic lines of cool jazz took over. Clubs like the Village Vanguard and the East Village Five Spot Cafe were the places to be, allowing poets, painters, actors, and musicians to cross-pollinate their ideas.

Acknowledgments

I would like to thank my editor, Christy Ottaviano—genie in a bottle, who not only has been a constant cheerleader and a thoughtful editor, but also a wish granter, allowing me to illustrate the novel from cover to cover!

I would like to thank my team at Macmillan, including Katie Klimowicz, who helped with the design and layout of this book.

Additionally, I would like to thank my teachers at Vermont College of Fine Arts, where I earned my MFA in Writing for Children and Young Adults. A very big thank-you goes to Mary Quattlebaum, who advised and guided me through the novel-writing process for this book, along with my other advisors: Betsy Partridge, Jane Kurtz, and Amanda Jenkins.

I owe a big thank-you to my agent, Carrie Hannigan, who believed in this manuscript and helped me put the finishing touches on it. Thank you for meeting with Christy for that fateful coffee before handing her the manuscript!

I'd like to thank Shannon Taggart, photographer, whose invitation to attend a séance was the initial spark for this novel. Thank you, Ralph Smith, Ginger Albertson, Caron Levis, Julia Hall, Jason Neufeld, Maria Falgoust, Tae Won Yu, and Jessica Grable for sharing dinner and drinks between working hours.

I'd like to thank my writer friends Caron Levis, Monica Rowe, Katie Bartlett, Bonnie Pipkin, and Monica Baker for all of their support and writing advice.

I'd like to thank Tracy Mantrone, librarian at the Clinton Hill branch of the Brooklyn Public Library, who has been my go-to for just about every question I can conjure.

Thank you, Hank Flacks and Jeff Corbin, for all of your advice and guidance. And last, a big thank-you to my parents and siblings for all of their support, lending an ear as I lamented every obstacle thrown my way on the path to publication.

About the Author

GILBERT FORD holds a BFA in illustration from Pratt Institute and an MFA in writing for children and young adults from Vermont College of Fine Arts. He is the author-illustrator of *How the Cookie Crumbled* and *The Marvelous Thing That Came from a Spring*, a Best STEM Book of the Year, as well as the illustrator of *Alice Across America*. The recipient of a Society of Illustrators Silver Medal, Gilbert marks his fiction debut with *The Mysterious Messenger*. He lives and works in Brooklyn, New York.

GILBERTFORD.COM